Maddy

Kate Petty was born in 1951, the youngest
of four children. Her own teenage years were
spent at a coeducational boarding-school,
before going on to York University. She
divides her working life between publishing
and writing. She lives in London with her
husband and teenage son and daughter.

The Girls Like You Quartet

Sophie
Hannah
Maddy
Charlotte

Maddy

KATE PETTY

Dolphin Paperbacks

These books are for Rachel, who approved

First published in Great Britain in 1999
as a Dolphin paperback
by Orion Children's Books
a division of the Orion Publishing Group Ltd
Orion House
5 Upper St Martin's Lane
London WC2H 9EA

A catalogue record for this book is
available from the British Library

Typeset at The Spartan Press Ltd,
Lymington, Hants
Printed in Great Britain by
Clays Ltd, St Ives plc

One

The whole holiday romance thing was my idea. Maybe it was a bit harsh, considering Charlotte's and Hannah's chances were practically zilch, but it certainly got them all talking at the sleepover. I was just so fed up with everything that was happening at home, and so looking forward to this holiday with Dad, that I wanted it to be totally perfect. And of course the perfect holiday means the perfect holiday romance.

My friends are great and I love them to bits, really I do, but I admit I sometimes feel envious of their nice little homes and their nice little families. Charlotte's mum even bakes cakes! My mum laughs about that sometimes when we're down to the pot noodles again. She says I'm lucky to look the way I do, considering how badly she feeds me, but since I've inherited her skinny figure I'm not complaining!

We had the sleepover at Sophie's on the last night of term. Sophie's my mate at school. Bit of an ice queen, all tall and blonde and blue-eyed, but we like the same things. She's much more intellectual than I am, though not as bright as Hannah. Hannah's a boffin, incredibly clever, and she's absolutely brilliant at music too. She goes to a posh all-girls' school, so she's a bit backward socially, if you

1

know what I mean. Charlotte's just plain shy. She could be really pretty if she lost some of her puppy fat. In fact she probably will lose it, because her sister was just the same, and you should see her now. Stunning! Charlotte definitely lives in her shadow.

Charlotte sort of started the romance idea, because she has the same holiday every year, poor cow, with her cousins in the Lake District. The only bright spot on that grey horizon seems to be a guy called Josh, who lives next door or something, and Charlotte has been madly in love with him for as long as I've known her. So we were talking about him and it made me think what a laugh it would be if we all decided to have a real holiday romance. No getting out of it because we'd all have to report back at the end. I've been watching the video of Pride and Prejudice for the millionth time and I still fancy the guy who plays Mr Darcy and I know that's the sort of guy I'm after. You know, a man, rather than a boy, or what passes for a boy at our school. Most of them are a complete waste of space. Ben Southwell's cute in an 'I'm so hard it hurts' sort of way, but we all know he's not hard at all really, though he is fit, and passionately in love with Sophie. I'm losing myself. Oh yes. I feel ready for a relationship with a man of the world. After all, I am almost fifteen.

I am going on the most fabulous holiday – with my dad, to Barbados! He's decided that he feels a bit sorry for me, what with Mum's latest, and anyway he's proud enough of me to go on holiday just him and me together. He's been to this place before and, although it's dead smart, it's apparently all super-friendly. He knows some people who'll be there already, and he's sure I'll meet up with loads of *other spoilt brats just like me. As if! He really hasn't got a clue how Mum and me and my little sister live. He spends at least six months a year in America because he's a script-writer – he goes 'where the bucks are' as he puts it. It was Mum who blew it as far as he was concerned, and I sometimes feel as if he's never forgiven me either, not that I had anything to do with it. I wanted him to stay. But he's pretty gorgeous, my dad, even though he's middle-aged. I can't wait to have him all to myself for a bit and to be his little princess again, just like in the old days.*

Of course, I didn't say all that to the others. It's exotic enough just to be going to Barbados. Especially when you compare it to Sophie camping in France and Hannah going on a music course. So I didn't want to go on about it too much. And after the video, the food, the thimblefuls of alcohol (I can't wait for that totally tropical banana daiquiri!) and giving each other makeovers – we made Hannah look amazing – we all went to sleep in our own little dreamworlds.

Mum goes around the whole time with a soppy smile on her face at the moment. She's permanently in a good mood, which is better than the permanent bad mood she was in six months ago, but I'm seriously beginning to think she's lost it. Eloise, that's my little sister, can't work out what's going on anyway, so she seems to be on another planet most of the time too. My family is bizarre, so I'd better explain it. Mum was married to my dad and they had me. When I was seven and in my first year at junior school – I remember it well because it's when I first met Sophie and Hannah and Charlotte – Mum fell in love with Gus. He converted Mum

3

into a feminist, socialist, green, ageing hippy sort of person, all ready to find herself. Up till then she'd been perfectly happy to forgo the stage and stay at home looking after me, while Dad went off to work and earned the money. Dad left us, furious, which was just so horrible, and Gus moved in. Mum had Gus and I had no one. Then, the icing on the cake, baby Eloise was born. Gus was much nicer then. He adored Eloise and was even a bit more understanding about me. I was a helpful kid, and Mum started to treat me more like a friend than a daughter. Her short-lived comeback went for a burton with a new baby to look after, so she was thrilled with all the dance and drama stuff that I did on Saturday mornings.

Cut to about a year ago, when Mum met Roddy. Compared with Roddy, Gus was a dream. But Roddy is a fitness freak and Gus was starting to get pretty flabby round the edges. Probably the home brew and surfing the Internet till all hours that did it. Then Roddy, who is a neighbour, came to fix the computer, encouraged Mum to go jogging – and that was it. Gus was out at work, Eloise and I were at school and Mum was left to get it on with Roddy. Gus moved out after some awful rows. Eloise was traumatised. Roddy hasn't moved in, thank God, because he only lives round the corner, but I suspect it's really because he's mean and doesn't want Mum to rely on him for money. Mum gets the odd bit of work doing tacky advertisements or voice-overs, but she hardly earns anything. Gus sends money for Eloise and Dad has always paid maintenance for me, but there isn't much dosh around right now. I actually earn quite a bit helping out with the little ones at the dance and drama place so I have enough for a few little luxuries.

Barbados is going to be the complete opposite. Mum and Eloise are ever so jealous, but I can't help that. Eloise is going to stay with the grandparents for a bit, so at least she'll have a nice time there. Dad's going to come and collect me at eight o'clock on Saturday morning, so instead of doing my normal Friday-night thing of going out late and then staying over with a friend, I'm in my room and packing.

I didn't have a suitcase so Mum borrowed one off Roddy. He's the sort of man to have a whole set of suitcases, one in every size. It's plain dark green but Eloise has stuck on some glittery little stickers from her collection to make it easier to pick out on the carousel. She says she and her friends were talking about it in the playground. Six-year-olds are so sophisticated these days! Eloise is a wonderfully adoring little sister. She loves all my make-up and clothes, so she was right there packing with me as if I was a Barbie doll in need of all the right outfits.

'You'll need lots of bikinis,' she said. 'And lots of nice dresses to wear to discos. And some shorts. And a nice outfit for dining.' I gave her a hug. Eloise and I can't quite get to grips with the 'dining' concept.

'You will bring me a present, won't you?' she said, as I released her.

'You bet!' I told her. It wasn't as if Gus was ever likely to take her on a glamorous holiday. It's lucky for him his parents live somewhere as exciting as Southend for Eloise to visit.

She soon got bored watching me folding my underwear and started playing with my make-up. She put on some red lipstick and started jigging about. 'Do that dance with me,

5

Maddy – the one they had on Top of the Pops?' She'd nearly worked it out on her own, amazing child, but I took her through it and we sang along as we did the steps. She watched, round-eyed, as I finished it off. I tried to do it just like the lead singer on TV. 'Co-ol!' said Eloise. 'That was so cool! Teach me the last bit, please!'

'Help me fold these things and then I will,' I said, being kind.

'Yuk, no! I'm not touching your smelly old knickers!' she said, and flounced out. Little sisters, eh? But I knew it was just because she was disappointed, and scared of me going away. I'm going to miss her too. I really, really love that kid.

She came back a few moments later with Mum. 'Oooh, you lucky thing,' said Mum, standing behind me and putting her arms round my neck. 'I wish I was going off on an exotic holiday. But not with Richard. And not the way I'm feeling. And someone needs to be with Eloise – don't they sweetheart?' Eloise had come round to join in our hug. I forgot for a moment how cross I was about vile Roddy and woolly old Gus. I adore my beautiful Mum – I just wish she wasn't so fickle about men. I don't intend to be. I see what Eloise is going through, with Gus leaving. At least she won't have to put up with a new baby, like I did. But then the baby did turn into Eloise, didn't it? And I wouldn't be without her for the whole world! 'Give Lo-lo a goodnight story, would you?' said Mum, 'and I'll check your packing.'

'Thanks Mum! Love you!' I said, giving her a kiss as Eloise tugged at my hand and pulled me towards her room.

Eloise snuggled down after I'd read her three stories and kissed every single one of her stuffed toys. Then she got up again and I took her through the last few steps of the dance, put her back into bed and kissed all the toys once more. Mum was zipping up my case when I went into my room. She got to her feet and stood with her hands resting in the small of her back. She straightened up when she saw me. 'There! I hope you've got enough of everything. Make Dad buy you things if you need them – he can afford it!' she said bitterly. 'Let's go down and have a cup of something and then you ought to get an early night.'

'Me?' I said. 'Not likely! I haven't watched Friday night TV for ages. I've got a lot of catching up to do.'

'In that case I might be in bed before you. I don't know why I'm so tired – but I'm exhausted for some reason.'

'Not seeing Roddy tonight, then, Mum?'

'No. I wanted to help you pack.'

'Well, you've done that. Come and watch telly with me instead.'

'Let's just do a final check of your journey bag. Camera?'

'Yes.'

'Passport?'

'Yes.'

'Book to read?'

'Lines for West Side Story to learn, yes.'

'When are the auditions?'

'As soon as we get back.' They're doing West Side Story at school next term, and if I don't get a part, I'll die. I'm OK on all the singing and dancing but it takes me a long time to learn lines. Oh, for the day when I can be in a movie and just do one short scene at a time! I was Tallulah in Bugsy Malone at primary school but Mum spent hours coaching me on the speaking part. She says she's just the same – a

7

good job she only has to say one or two words for her adverts! In the last one she just had to say, 'Mmmm! Soft!' Even I wouldn't find that too taxing! Songs are different – I don't have a problem with words when I'm singing them. Of course, I really want to be Maria . . .

'Sun lotion, Nurofen?'

'Yes, yes.'

'And what are you wearing for the journey?'

'These thin trousers and this top and these sandals.' I pointed to them laid out over my chair. 'And this jacket with all my important documents in the inside pocket.'

'That's my girl.'

'Let's watch telly. Tea or coffee? I'll make it.'

'Tea would be brilliant. I don't seem to fancy coffee at the moment.' She flopped down on the sofa with that daft smile on her face again.

Next morning Dad arrived at eight o'clock on the dot. He turned up on the doorstep looking all tanned and handsome and pleased with himself. 'Hi there, princess! You all ready then?' I threw my arms round him. I hadn't seen him for four months – we'd arranged all this by phone. Dad's a mobile-phone freak and likes to call up from all the weirdest places he can think of. ('Maddy – it's me. Guess where I'm calling from?'

'The toilet, Dad.'

'No,' etc. It's pretty childish if you ask me.)

Mum came to the door. Mum and Dad used to be really frosty with each other, and then they were very formal but now they act like friends. 'Have you got time to come in for coffee, or are you racing to catch the plane?' As Mum spoke,

Eloise peeped round her, shyly. She used to know Dad as someone who was always angry with Mum (though never with her), so she's always unsure of herself when he turns up.

Dad crouched down to her level – 'Ello, Ello-ise!' he said (Dad-type joke). But then he straightened up and looked at his watch and told Mum we ought to be getting going. So out of habit I went upstairs to the loo (before a journey) while they had a few words together, gave Lo-lo a final hug and told her to be good, came down for my case and followed Dad out to the flashy hire car he had for the journey to the airport (I hoped at least one of my friends might walk by at that moment, but of course it was too early for them). Then Mum kissed me goodbye and we were off, leaving Mum and Eloise to wave us into the distance.

'Excited?' Dad asked as we turned the corner and left them behind.

'Can't wait,' I told him. 'I can't believe today has really come, I've been looking forward to it for so long.'

'You won't be disappointed, I promise. So how's school been?' Absent fathers always feel they have to ask this.

'OK. I get by. Guess what – they're auditioning for West Side Story at the beginning of next term.'

'Maria, then, at the very least!'

'Glad we agree on that. I've got it with me to learn.'

'Good girl. Very dedicated. Though I want you to have a good holiday. Carefree. Forget about your troubles at home.'

Now, I can talk about it being bad at home, but at the end of the day, it's Mum I'm loyal to, and I don't want Dad jumping to conclusions. 'As long as we don't talk about Mum, Dad. Let's just say, of course I want a great holiday. And it will be, won't it?'

9

'It'll be great as long as this prat lets me get past him.' Dad concentrated on driving after that and we barely spoke again until we'd handed over the car at the airport. We flew a lot when it was Mum, Dad and me, but I've hardly even been to Heathrow since then, so I'd forgotten just how exciting it is. So many people from so many different countries all speaking different languages. Little kids charging about. Old people looking bewildered. Cool students. A whole group of American pensioners in yellow baseball caps. Dad grabbed a trolley and I kept close to him. He smiled at me. 'It's a long time since I've been accompanied by a girl who turns so many heads,' he said after a couple of guys whistled at me (I'm so used to it I don't notice any more). 'I can see I'm going to have to fight off the young men while we're away. Well, they'd better be afraid, very afraid, that's all I can say, when my daughter's virtue is at stake.'

'Gee, thanks, Dad.' So where has he been for the last two years whenever guys have come on to me? All those last-night after-show parties? My maths teacher? Robbie, my ex? Don't say it, Maddy, don't say it. We were queuing to check in and I didn't want an argument.

It didn't help when the guy at the check-in desk did a double-take at the date of birth in my passport. 'I had you down for seventeen at least,' he said with a charming smile and then pulled himself up short when he realised that the fierce-looking man behind me was my father. When we'd handed over our luggage, Dad and I had at least an hour to kill before our flight was called. We wandered round the shops and he bought me all sorts of bits in the Body Shop and three magazines. If Over-Protective Dad was the price I had to pay for Generous Dad then maybe it was worth it.

At last we were called and went through to the departure lounge. I remember waving my dad off so many times when I was little and wondering where he disappeared to. I'd imagined the departure lounge as a lounge in the sky with sofas made of clouds. But no. Just the usual seats and a duty-free shop. Oh wow! The perfume counter of my dreams and all at duty-free prices. 'I'm going to get a bottle of whisky,' said Dad. 'Do you want something smelly by Dior or someone?'

Do I! Something smelly by Tommy Hilfiger or Calvin Klein or Issey Miyake would do me just fine. 'Are you sure Dad? I mean, I'd love just a little bottle of toilet water.'

'Fine. Choose what you want and bring it over.' I wandered up and down, squirting scent on my wrists. Aftershave too. How to choose? I've kept going on those little Issey Miyake testers you get handed out in the shopping mall recently, but a whole bottle! I went for the Hugo Boss in the end.

Finally, finally it was time to board. It was all just so romantic – the whine of the engines, the bustle of people settling in their seats, doing up their seat belts, muffled voices. Dad had got me a window seat so I sat and watched all the last minute stuff on the tarmac. I was just so excited – it was impossible to be cool.

And then we were taxiing along to the runway. I had a moment of sheer, delicious terror and then we were whizzing faster and faster down the runway and up, up. That awful moment when the plane seems to hang in the air before it straightens out and then a wonderful normality as the air hostesses do their stuff and the journey really seems to get underway. What a buzz! Who could need anything else!

It's a long haul to Barbados – eight and three-quarter hours. I felt I knew the people sitting around us pretty well by the end of it. There was an unforgettable family who were heading for the same hotel as us. I would have noticed them anyway because they were a good-looking couple with a little girl the same age as Lo-lo, called Bianca. Bianca's a stunning kid, apart from the fact that most of her hair has fallen out. In fact, I discovered, she's got leukaemia and this will almost certainly be their last family holiday. It's so sad and so unfair. She's a great kid. I read to her quite a bit – she had lots of the same books as Eloise, and I said it would be nice to do things with her once we're there, too. Give her parents a break. Dad kept saying, 'Don't get too involved,' but I wanted to.

One more thing about the journey. The film was a 15. Dad seems to forget that I will be fifteen in just over a month. A few bare breasts on show (no worse than the changing rooms at school) and he went frantic. 'Why on earth are they showing such rubbish! They ought to show a family film!' Which is ridiculous because he enjoys a good movie, and certainly wouldn't be happy with The Lion King, I know. It was quite funny – every time there was a faintly saucy bit he coughed a lot and said, 'I don't think you should be watching this, you know.' Does he really think I'm that innocent? Don't I have to put up with Mum and Roddy in the next room? – but that's hardly something I'd discuss with Dad. As I said, he doesn't have a clue how we live.

We ate and dozed and read and ate and chatted and dozed the strange long day away. It felt like a lifetime before the captain's voice was telling us that we were coming in to land and we could see the edge of the island appearing through the clouds as we bumped down through them. And there was Barbados – small and green, encircled by a ring of white sand and turquoise sea. Wow.

Two

The first thing you notice about Barbados, apart from the warmth which hits you like the blast from a fan heater as soon as you get off the plane, is how like England it is! Our taxi from the airport was like a minibus with a lovely, smiley driver and we drove for three-quarters of an hour down quite narrow lanes past English-looking churches and cricket pitches and golf courses and big old country houses. We went through one town but most of the time we had the sea to our left and hills to our right. They even drive on the left here! But the sky was a gorgeous blue with lots of little fluffy clouds and the flowers were all bright colours and the trees were palm trees. And the sea! That was pretty *un*-English! Dad was like a kid he was so excited, and kept pointing things out to me. 'That's a sugar plantation over there! Look at the little wooden houses! That's where we will go down in a submarine! Look at the catamarans!' I caught myself wishing Mum and Eloise were with us, but then I was *so* glad that I was thousands of miles away from the odious Roddy.

13

It was getting pretty glitzy as we travelled up the west coast. Barbados is only 21 miles top to bottom. There's about ten miles of sandy beach with all those fabulous hotels and swimming pools and beach bars along it. My main impression was of great stretches of blue sky, blue sea and white sand, dotted about with colourful flowers and umbrellas and sails. Southend it isn't!

'We're coming up to our hotel now,' said Dad. I saw this beautiful old pink stone house surrounded by a cluster of buildings with tiled roofs, and two huge swimming pools. Posh, or what?

It was late afternoon, early evening, Barbados time when we checked into the hotel. It was beautifully cool after the heat outside. I looked around the reception area for Bianca and her parents, but I suppose it had taken a while for them to sort out her wheelchair and things like that. Dad, with his tan and trendy shades, looked quite at home here, but *I* felt like something the cat brought in! I felt so scruffy, and as for my case with little glittery stickers all over it standing next to my scabby old schoolbag – well, I wished Roddy had been spared the trouble of lending it. I was glad when we were led away to our very own, completely wondrous two-bedroom suite (*suite*!) where I could dump my bags, thrown open the French windows and gaze across the tropical gardens to the beach. It was almost like having our own apartment, with its own front door, a small sitting room with a balcony and a bedroom off each side.

Dad definitely had the 'master' bedroom with its

own balcony, its own TV and a vast double bed. Mine was smaller with two single beds and my own 'en suite'. No balcony, but I wasn't complaining. I unpacked straight away and made it all cosy. I like to keep my room at home nice and tidy anyway and this was far too beautiful to mess up. The hotel had put vases of flowers around and the bathroom was full of all sorts of freebies. There was another TV in the sitting room and – get this – our own mini-bar. 'Hey, go easy on the mini-bar!' Dad said. 'The tap-water is perfectly drinkable. We don't want to run up unnecessary bills on the bottled stuff.'

'Do you mean I can't help myself to a pina colada, Dad?'

'Certainly not, my girl!' But he isn't really mean, my dad. 'Go on, have a coke or something – since it's your first ever experience of a mini-bar – and some of those chocolate things if you want. I'm going to have a quick shower – and then we'll go and see what's what.'

'I'm ever so tired, Dad. Can't I just pig out on these things and sit in front of the TV for a bit?'

'Take a tip from an experienced traveller, love. Try and make it through to bed Barbados-time so that you don't wake up in the night and then you'll be fine. It's only four hours different – or is it five with summer-time? Well, maybe you can go to bed at ten instead of eleven. Sit for a bit and then freshen up and change into one of your little dresses – we can hit the beach restaurant and watch the sunset. How does that sound?'

'Fab.' I put my feet up, punched the remote and found MTV.

'Come on, sweetheart. I want to see that sunset and drink that rum. What's taking you so long? Don't you look gorgeous enough already?' I was wearing my little O'Neill surfy dress and trainers – understated but sexy, I thought – and I was just putting the finishing touches to my make-up. I made kissy faces at myself in the mirror. 'Call me old-fashioned,' said Dad, 'but I didn't think fourteen-year-olds wore make-up.'

'Do fourteen-year-olds wear make-up, Dad! Is the Pope a whatsit – and do bears, you know, in the woods?'

'Sorry, sorry. I've obviously got a lot to learn. But do get a move on.'

I gave myself a last appraising look in the mirror. I've got quite a cat-like face and my eyes are a funny goldy colour – tawny, is how Mum describes them. My hair is annoyingly wavy, nearly shoulder-length and the same sort of colour. I describe myself as honey-blonde, but somehow I've inherited Dad's dark eyelashes and tanned skin. OK. Quick splash of the Hugo Boss and we're off.

The restaurant is a short walk away through the tropical garden. It was dark and cool inside but the arches at the front were open on to a terrace bar that overlooked the beach and the setting sun. 'Let's go to the bar first,' said Dad, and led me past the tables to the terrace. I thought of Lo-lo and my 'dining outfit' – these people were *so* dressed up. My dress is new and so are my trainers – Dad broke in on my observations. 'Dressy lot, aren't they? But nothing beats a stunning girl simply dressed. I've got that heads-turning sensation again, last felt when I was first married to your mother!'

'I can't help it, Dad.'

'I know you can't – I'll just have to cope, won't I?' and he gave me his adorable worried bassett-hound look. He used to do that when he teased me and I told him off – '*naughty* daddy' – when I was little.

'Have you seen anyone you know yet?' I asked him.

'Not yet. I think they're coming in a couple of days.' He looked away. 'Now, tell me what you want to drink and then I'll get us a couple of menus to peruse.' I perched myself on a bar stool and faced the sunset. I was totally confused about what time it was – hardly surprising since it felt like midnight but was in fact about seven, in which case it seemed far too early for the sun to be setting.

I mentioned this to Dad when he brought me my drink. Before he had time to answer, the guy sitting next to me started off about tropical sunsets. Then he held out his hand to Dad – 'Brian Hayter. Here for the golf you know. You a golfer?'

'Richard Dumont. Well, yes, as a matter of fact,' said Dad.

'Does your wife play?' He looked at me. I felt a giggle starting.

Dad kept a straight face. 'My wife and I are separated. This is my daughter, Madeleine. She's fourteen.' Thanks, Dad. Make sure everybody knows.

'Sorry, old chap. They all look so grown-up these days. And my wife – well, you know, a little nip and tuck here, not to mention the hair colour stuff. Hard to tell the difference.'

We were soon given the opportunity to see what he meant when three women appeared. They were dressed similarly in little designer numbers, but the two daughters looked almost identical, one was brown-haired and horsy and the other red-haired and horsy. 'Girls!' said Brian. 'Madeleine, meet Cordelia and Flavia. Richard, this is my wife, Gina.' We all shook hands. Gina lit up a very long cigarette in a holder and proceeded to flirt with Dad.

'Not *the* Richard Dumont!' was her chat-up line. I must remember that.

The girls stood and talked to me. They held identical complicated drinks full of fruit and umbrellas and straws. 'I'm Flavia,' said the flame-haired one. 'People think we're twins, worse luck, but I'm older than she is.'

'It's not as if we even have the same colour hair!' said Cordelia. But you have identical noses and chins, I wanted to say, but, hey! Here were some people more or less my age. I was going to have to start somewhere.

'Have you been to Barbados before?' I asked them.

'Last four years. Same hotel,' said Flavia, yawning.

'You'll have to tell me what to do,' I said.

'Well, we ride and go to the races,' said Cordelia. Hardly surprising.

'And get sloshed!' said Flavia, with a whinnying laugh.

'Jonty does watersporty things,' said Cordelia. 'He's

our little brother. A complete pain.' This was hardly encouraging.

Dad stood up. 'Maddy and I haven't eaten yet,' he told the Hayters. 'Would you excuse us if we go to the restaurant now?'

'Golly,' said Gina. 'You must be harry starvers. Let them go, Brian, you old bore. I'm sure we can all meet up again later, and girls, you'll be able to show Madeleine the ropes, won't you?'

I was really beginning to flag. Even the gorgeous food seemed like a huge effort. 'The golf's really good here,' said Dad. *Riveting.* I remembered why my friends try to spend as little time in public with their parents as possible.

'I don't know what Mum will say when I tell her you've taken up golf,' I teased him.

'It's a good game. I wouldn't mind a few rounds with old Brian over there one of these days. D'you fancy tagging along with old Flavi*ah* and Cordeli*ah*?' he put on a lah-di-dah voice.

'You know me, Dad. I'm not that fussy about the company. But don't you think they're a bit old for me? They "get sloshed"'! I mimicked Flavia's voice.

'Do they indeed? And they don't look half as glam as you do. How old do you think they are?'

'By my reckoning they're about fifteen and eighteen.'

But Dad was miles away. 'It must be expensive bringing a whole family here.'

'Something tells me they can afford it, Dad, don't you think?'

It was almost completely dark by the time we had finished eating. Dad was all for heading back to the bar, but my insides were swilling with Coke enough already, and I could really barely keep my eyes open. 'I'll come back to our rooms with you, sweetheart. You must forgive me, I'm not used to looking after a teenage daughter yet. I forget how young you are.'

'Just tired, Dad. I don't need looking after – honest. But I do need to sleep.' We were walking back through the tropical gardens. It was discreetly lit with lanterns and filled with an extraordinary chirping noise. 'What's that noise? It never seems to go away.'

'Tree frogs,' said Dad. 'You soon get used to them. They go on all night – rather fun aren't they?'

There was another bar just off the reception foyer. I couldn't understand why anyone would want to have a drink with*out* a view of the bay when you could have a drink with one, but it was livelier right now than the one we'd left. Dad turned towards the bar where people were definitely gathering around one man. 'Gracious!' Dad nudged me. 'That's—'

But at the same time I was nearly knocked off my feet by a high-speed wheelchair with a little girl in it. 'Maddy!' she called. 'You're here in time to read me a bedtime story!' It was Bianca of course. She sounded just like Eloise.

'Hi Bianca!' I crouched down to be at her level. 'Listen, I'm *really, really* tired right now, because I didn't get any sleep on the plane like you did. So will you let me off, just this one time?'

Bianca's mum chipped in. 'Poor Maddy, Bianca.

Look, she's yawning! Don't worry, Maddy. She's getting quite spoilt by all this attention!'

'I don't really mind,' said Bianca. 'Night-night Maddy!' and she threw her arms round my neck and gave me a good night kiss.

'Does she always kiss strangers?' I asked her mum, laughing as I tried to break free.

'Usually,' she said, cheerfully.

I stood up and looked for Dad. I could see him hovering on the edge of the group gathered around an imposing blond guy with designer stubble and trendy specs, very goodlooking in a rich and famous forty-something way. It was an incredible sight – really like bees round a honeypot (or wasps round a Coke can, in my experience). There was a distinct *buzz!* Dad looked round and I caught his eye. He beckoned me over, so I waved goodnight to Bianca and went to persuade Dad that I absolutely *had* to go to bed. He grabbed my arm and whispered in my ear – or shouted, rather, 'It's Oliver O'Neill!'

'*The* Oliver O'Neill?' Of course I had heard of him – he's only about the most famous film director there is. 'Don't you think the poor guy wants to get away from his adoring fans on holiday, Dad? Anyway, I want to go to *sleep*!'

'They're his friends,' said Dad. 'Some of them were here last year. He's the sort of guy who just loves an audience. And I think half of them are family. He pays for them to come here, I gather.'

'Ssh, Dad. I'm sure they don't want that broadcast!'

'Oh, all right, little Miss Bossy,' he said fondly,

turning his back on the group. 'But I do know his son is here. He's got one of those ridiculous hippy names. Called after a tree. Linden – no – that's the daughter. Redwood, or something.' Now he was no longer drowned out by the people in the bar, his voice rang out.

'Did someone mention my name?' Oh my God. There, blocking our way, stood a drop-dead gorgeous, sun-tanned, sun-bleached teenage guy with an infectious smile and perfect Californian teeth. Totally unabashed, he reached out and shook Dad's hand. 'Hi! I'm Red O'Neill.' He grinned at me. 'O'Neill, as advertised on your dress!'

'Richard Dumont,' said Dad, quite used to this sort of friendly American courtesy, even from a teenager. 'And Maddy – who's suffering from jet-lag and about to be put to bed.' I smiled up under my lashes at this *divine* boy – around sixteen or seventeen, I'd say – and decided to look no further for my holiday romance.

Three

My body clock told me it was practically lunch time when I woke up, but of course it was only half-past seven in the morning! I stayed in bed, listening to the waves breaking on the sand. I couldn't really believe I was finally in Barbados – I've been dreaming about it for *so* long. I lay there for about an hour, just thinking about the journey and the people in the hotel. I feel really involved with Bianca already, of course. And I'm curious about horsy old Flavia and Cordelia. Perhaps they're not so bad – and it would be good to have some other teenagers to muck about with.

And then of course, there's Red. Hmm. Perhaps he's already got a girlfriend, but I don't think so, somehow. There was a sort of jolt of electricity – of recognition – when we first saw one another. He seemed kind of *familiar*. About the right height, too. Nice mouth. Hunky – must do some kind of sport. Good cheek-bones.

It was no good. I was *wide* awake. I just had to get up. I had a shower. It was lovely. All that free shower gel and shampoo. Checked myself out in my bikini. Fine, fine. One of the others – Hannah, or was it Charl? – once said that I had the sort of seamless body that never looked indecent, even when I had nothing on. I didn't know what she meant at first, but now I do, and I realise I'm lucky. Some girls seem to be made of all sorts of bits joined together, rather than all of a piece, especially if they tan unevenly. My skin goes a uniform golden brown, about the same colour as my hair and eyes. I'm not super-tall or top-heavy, or extra-anything, really. So, what I'm getting at, is that I don't feel embarrassed in any way when I'm wearing a bikini, just comfortable. I put some shorts and a blouse on over it.

I dried my hair and did my face – unblock those pores before I load on the Factor 15. I arranged my hair to cover my ears. They're my only major hang-up.

They stick out more than I like. Just a subtle touch of make up and I was ready for my breakfast. There was juice in the mini-bar and fruit in the bowl, but I wanted real food. I went into our living room. No sign of Dad of course. I put my ear to his door. I could hear him snoring! Thank God we don't have to listen to that at home! I opened the French windows onto the balcony. There was the sea! I could see a few families – mostly with young kids, it has to be said, making their way towards the dining room. Perhaps Bianca's family would be there. Anyway, I was starving. There was some hotel notepaper and a pencil, so I left a note for Dad –

> Morning Sleepyhead!
> Gone to EAT.
> See U later.
> Maddy x x x x

I felt a bit peculiar going on my own, but I figured that I'd soon discover the crowd, and I certainly didn't intend doing everything with an aged parent. And it was fine. There was a huge breakfast table groaning with jugs of fruit juice and fresh fruit and rolls and yoghurts and croissants and pancakes and waffles where everybody helped themselves. I poured some fruit juice, filled a bowl with chunks of pineapple and mango and peach and yoghurt, and surveyed the dining room, looking for somewhere to sit. There was no sign of Bianca and her parents, but to my surprise someone was waving from the terrace near the bar.

It was a girl with brown hair pulled up into a topknot and wearing a sundress. She was sitting with a boy of about fourteen. I walked some way towards them with my breakfast before I realised that it was Cordelia. Somehow she looked much more normal on her own and with her hair off her face – not all dolled up. The boy must be the brother – the 'pain'.

Cordelia pulled out a chair for me. 'Good! You're another early bird! I can't understand people who waste half the day in bed. Shove over, Jonty. Make room for – what was your name again? Call me Dilly, by the way. People only call me Cordelia when they're angry with me.'

I sat down. 'Maddy. Thanks, Dilly. Hi, Jonty. I just haven't got used to the time change yet. And it all seems so brilliant here. I can't wait to find out what's going on.'

'Depends what you're into,' said Jonty. 'The girls like riding, but I'm really into watersports – so there's masses to do here. Have you ever done any?'

'A bit of surfing,' I said casually. (I have, on a school journey to Dorset.) Anyway, dancers are quick learners at that sort of thing.

'Plenty of that here!' he said.

'Maddy won't want to go round with a fourteen-year-old!' said Dilly. I kept quiet on this one.

'Maybe Maddy's not like you!' said Jonty. 'If she likes watersports she won't mind who she does it with. Anyway, there's an entire school cricket team down there every morning at the moment, and they're all fifteen.'

Dilly perked up. 'Really? Why didn't you tell me?'

'I don't tell you everything. Anyway, you and the Flavour aren't interested in what I tell you.'

'A *whole* cricket team, did you say?'

'Hardly likely to be half of one. They're from some day school in London.'

'That's where I'm from,' I said.

'Lucky you,' said Dilly. 'We live in the sticks. And go to boarding-school.'

'Not the *same* boarding-school!' said Jonty, as if it was out of the question that boys and girls should be educated together.

'London's cool,' I said, and decided not to talk about schools. 'So when do you start, Jonty?'

'Soon,' he said. 'Do you want to come?'

'Why not?' I said. 'I'll have to make contact with my dad first, though, so he knows where I am. Are you coming, Dilly?'

'Not today,' said Dilly. 'I'm stuck with Flavia. She's got plans. *When* she gets up. She fancies this bloke, so she wants to hang around the pool in case he goes down there. He's American. And good-looking.

'And won't be the slightest bit interested in our hideous sister,' said Jonty.

'Jonty!' said Dilly, suddenly loyal. 'But you're right,' she added, all loyalty instantly evaporating. 'Still, perhaps he'll be interested in me.'

'You're ugly, too!' said Jonty, and ducked. I thought he was pushing it a bit, but I don't have brothers, so I wouldn't know. Anyway, Dilly certainly isn't as plain as Flavia.

Dilly cuffed him and smiled at me. 'Told you he was a pain. Younger brothers are just so *rude*. No respect for their elders and betters.'

We all stood up. 'Meet you in the bar in half an hour,' said Jonty. 'You have to go on a banana boat even if we can't book you in for anything else.'

'He's right,' said Dilly wistfully. 'Wish I hadn't promised Flavia now. Never mind. See you later!'

I walked back through the tropical gardens to our rooms. The day was hotting up but there was quite a breeze rustling the leaves. I let myself in quietly, in case Dad was still sleeping. Far from it. As soon as I came through the door he *roared* at me – it gave me quite a shock – 'Where on *earth* have you been? I've been searching the rooms for you (yeah, Dad, all three of them)! How dare you just disappear like that?'

Deep breath. He probably has a hangover. I calmly pointed out my note and answered him really soothingly. 'I just went for breakfast, Dad. I've been awake for ages, and I was starving.'

'You went on your own?'

'Why not?'

'Well – how can I look after you if I don't know where you are?'

'I left you a note, Dad – and I'm not a kid any more. I do all sorts of things on my own, you know – go to school, go shopping, go out—'

'All right, all right. But I'm just not used to this.'

'As you said earlier, Dad.'

'Well, it's true. We'll have to come to some sort of arrangement.'

'Precisely. After all, you didn't feel the need to tell me exactly where you were last night, did you?'

'I was in the bar.'

'I wasn't to know that.'

'Well, it's different, I'm grown up.'

'Not that different, Dad.'

'But I want us to do things together.'

'Uh-huh. Like playing golf?'

'OK sweetheart. I see what you're getting at. What shall we do today then?'

'Well, I'd sort of planned on going down to do watersports with someone.'

'*Someone*?' He was shouting again.

'Calm down, Dad. With Jonty, the Hayters' son. It's all laid on by the hotel, all supervised. Why don't you come too?'

It clearly wasn't Dad's idea of fun. Trip round the bay maybe, but nothing too energetic. Mum would have been the opposite – she's willing to try anything. 'No, you go darling, and I'll meet you back here at lunch-time. You're sure you won't come to any harm? I thought I might sit by the pool this morning. See who's here, plan some outings . . .'

I packed a towel and sun lotion, found my shades and gave Dad a hug. 'Don't worry about me Daddy. I'm only doing the same as you, really. I'm just more energetic. I'm sure I'll be quite safe with Jonty. See you at lunch time. Breakfast's brilliant by the way. Oh, and can I have some money, in case I have to buy anything?'

Dad reached into his pocket for a few dollars. 'Here you are. Now, *lunch-time*, OK?'

'Thanks, Daddy.' I gave him a hug. 'Love you!'

Poor old Dad. But he really has to learn that he can't go away for seven years and suddenly expect to boss me about when he chooses to come back into my life.

Jonty was waiting for me. He doesn't have the same horsy looks as his sisters and mother. He was a carbon copy – with hair – of his bland dad. 'Face like a smacked bottom' as Sophie would put it – kind of squashed up and surprised looking. He's OK though. I wouldn't want to introduce him to some of the lads at school, but no one was asking me to. 'I like your shades,' he said.

We wound our way down to the beach under the palms and past the vast swimming-pool. I hadn't realised just how enormous it was. It curved round several bends of the hotel, with shops and kiosks all down one side of it. Parts of it were almost hidden by brightly flowering bushes, and others were splashy with fountains and cascades. Some families were already out there under the sun umbrellas and there were plenty of children swimming. It seemed odd to me to have a pool when the sea was right there. I suppose it's all within the hotel grounds and it means people never need to go any further. What kind of people would choose that?

Jonty seemed to read my thoughts. 'I really like being down on the beach,' he said. 'We've been coming to this place for years, and I'm just bored with the hotel. Weyhey! Here comes a banana boat! You'll love this!'

When he'd first said 'banana boat', I'd thought he meant a traditional West Indian banana boat, for shipping bananas, but oh no! This was a boat *that looked like a banana!* A local guy brought it up on to the beach. People gathered around him.

'We won't get on this one,' said Jonty, 'but we'll be at the front of the queue for the next one. Just watch this time.'

'What about our clothes? Those people are wearing swimsuits.'

'You'll see why. Sorry. I forgot. Some of my mates are over there under that beach umbrella. Give me your bag and I'll get them to look after it. You stay here in the queue.' I stripped down to my bikini, bunged my stuff in my bag and watched Jonty make his way over to a group of boys – no doubt the cricket team. There were some girls with them too. 'If that's the cricket team,' I asked Jonty when he came back, 'who are the girls?'

'Sisters, and daughters of the staff, apparently. They're staying in chalets somewhere over there,' he said loftily and pointed into the distance. 'You haven't escaped their attention either. I'll have to introduce you after our ride. They have to be better company than my vile sisters!' But I wasn't really listening. I was watching the kids on the banana boat. They sat astride it and were towed off into the waves, curving round across the bay. Everyone fell off, but the water was so shallow they just stood up and tried to climb back on when it came past. Cool!

'It's coming back now,' said Jonty. 'Are you ready?'

'You bet!' We paid our money and climbed on. The water was warm and wonderful. The other kids were quite little – they made me wonder if it was something Bianca could manage if I helped her – and we were off. Aaagh! I fell off almost straight away! I stood up again and Jonty managed to haul me back on. I held on tighter this time, but then, just before the end, the driver did a particularly vicious U-turn and three of us tumbled into the sea. 'He always does that,' said Jonty. 'No point in getting back on.' We slooshed our way through the shallows back to the beach. He looked at his posh watersports watch. 'I've got windsurfing in twenty minutes,' he said. 'Do you want to see if you can join in today or shall we sign you up for tomorrow?'

'I don't know, Jonty. Is there anywhere I can find out exactly what's on offer and then decide?'

'Of course,' said Jonty, gallantly. He is quite a sweetheart, I can tell. 'Tell you what. Come and meet this shower. They won't all be windsurfing.' We walked across the hot white sand to where the group were sprawled out together under beach umbrellas on sunbeds and towels.

'Hey, Jont!' called one of the boys. 'Where did you find this gorgeous creature?' (He was a smarmy one – I'd have to watch out for him.)

'This is Maddy,' said Jonty. 'She only got here yesterday, so we have to show her what's what – save her from my sisters.'

'Hi,' I said, and stood looking at them. There was

indeed an entire cricket team from a London school, most of them leering at me in that embarrassed but friendly way boys have, as if each and every one of them is saying – *I'm* the one you ought to be interested in because *I'm* much fitter/cooler/more intelligent/better-endowed/richer/etc. than the others . . . At first glance none of them attracted me in *that* way – they were simply too gauche, but I'm always ready to be friends. The few girls were more interesting. They looked at me in that coolly appraising way *girls* have. Hmmm, OK so you're pretty, but you're probably a complete bitch without any brains and your hair's definitely dyed and you've almost certainly got tissues in your bra. You know the sort of thing. All except one. She stood up and came over to me. 'Hi, Maddy,' she said, her accent distinctly American. 'I'm Linden O'Neill. Red – my brother – told me about you.'

She was shorter than me, probably about my age, though she could have been a year younger or older. It was impossible to tell because she seemed so poised. 'Hi,' I said. 'I only *just* saw Red last night. I was dead on my feet!'

'Well, you made quite an impression!' she said. 'He told me all about this stunning English girl he'd just met.'

I smiled inwardly at this. It was good news, but right now I wanted to make friends with the crowd. Red could wait. Jonty was in a hurry to go windsurfing and several of the cricketers and their sisters were going too. I asked him where my towel and things were. 'Over here!' said Mr Smarm, waving. So I had to go over to him. Linden came with me. 'I'm Charles,' he said. 'You two could be sisters – did you know that?' Linden and I looked at each other and laughed.

'Well, we're not,' she said. 'Charles, give Maddy her stuff, you greaseball!' Charles pretended to look hurt as he handed over my bag. 'Now,' said Linden. 'We're going to sit as far away from him as possible,' and led me away with a backwards grin at Charles. 'He's OK,' she said. 'Just bigheaded. With an ego that needs a few holes putting in it. I know he comes on strong to me because of my father being famous and everything and I *so* don't like that!'

We sat down with the other girls. 'You must be very rich if you're in that hotel!' said one of the little ones.

'Shut up, Abby,' said another girl who must have been her older sister. 'Excuse her,' she said to me. 'We're only here because our dad's a teacher at the school which brought the cricket team and my mum can't stop going on about how much money everyone else must have. Why she can't just enjoy the perks of Dad's job I don't know. I certainly can. I'm Holly, by the way. Another tree, aren't I Linden?'

I liked the look of Holly. She's got long, dark, pre-Raphaelite hair and big bright eyes. 'I'm staying there with my dad,' I said. 'He and Mum are divorced. Mum and me and my little sister live in mortal terror of the gas bill and Dad comes on holiday to places like this.' I didn't want them getting the wrong impression. 'Not that *I'm* complaining.'

'Our hotel is something else, though, isn't it?' said Linden. 'They even tell you how to dress – "elegantly casual" is what it says in the brochure! Can you believe that? You know, there are some women there who change their bikinis three times a day, I swear. Oh yes, and not just their bikinis – the matching sarongs and headscarves as well.' She has a nice grin, like her brother's. 'We're on the single-dad guilt trip too – but that's been the story of our whole Hollywood little lives. That's why I like you British guys – you're just so down-to-earth and – normal!'

'Gee, thanks, Linden,' said Holly.

I suddenly felt the need to defend Dad. 'Dad wasn't the guilty party in my parents' divorce,' I told them. 'It was my Mum who left him. Mum's great though.' I wanted to defend her too. It was strange sharing all this stuff with people I barely knew.

'My mom's a saint,' said Linden. 'That's why Red and I aren't too *ab*normal I guess. She's always been there. But with a dad like ours – you'd have to be a saint.'

'What do you mean?' asked Holly. 'God, my family seems so *bor*ing!'

'Boring is good, trust me,' said Linden. 'Ever heard of the casting couch?' Holly and I nodded. 'It's where Dad spends his life when he's not actually directing, if you get my meaning. Not at all nice, and – before we go any further – let me say, keep out of his way! You might want a part in his teenage movie version of *West Side Story* – but believe me, you don't want it *that* much. He is *shame*less where women of any age are concerned, totally without morals. Amusing, clever, yes. But strictly for the grown-ups. I tell you, I don't let my friends near him.'

'That's awful!' said Holly, sounding very British and shocked. I could see Abby looking round-eyed next to her.

'*Hollywood*'s awful,' said Linden. She stood up abruptly.

I couldn't believe what I'd just heard. 'I'm auditioning for our school production of *West Side Story*!' I said. 'What a coincidence!'

'Our school's doing that this year, too,' said Holly. 'Not really coincidence – it's on the music syllabus.'

'Stick to school productions!' said Linden. 'Movies suck!'

Then Linden, Holly and Abby were looking at me. 'Banana boat?' said Holly.

'Come *on*,' said Abby, tugging at her arm. 'We won't get on it if we don't hurry!'

'Try and stop me,' I said, and followed them.

Linden and I walked back past the swimming-pool. Even from a distance we could see my dad and Brian Hayter at the poolside. Ma Hayter and the girls weren't far away. And there, crouched beside Flavia, was Red. Something clicked. Of course, Flavia's handsome American – Red. I even felt a pang of something. Jealousy?

'That girl!' said Linden. 'Now does she really think she stands a chance with my adorable brother? Jonty's OK, but her! Her hair's a fabulous colour but she looks kinda horsy. She's not even nice!' Linden looked at me. 'Uh-oh! She's not your friend is she?'

'I only got here yesterday,' I reminded her. 'And that's my dad with them.'

'That would explain Red, then,' said Linden. 'Probably asking your dad where you are. He doesn't waste time, my brother. Let's go and join them. I can't wait to see her face when you come along – or Red's for that matter. Hang on – watch this.' She delved into her bag for her mobile and tapped out a number. We could just hear another phone warbling in the distance and I saw Red reaching into the back pocket of his shorts. 'Red?' said Linden. 'Be prepared, brother dear. Guess who's coming to dinner!' She folded up the phone and grinned at me triumphantly. 'There!' she said. 'Didn't I say their faces would be a picture?'

Four

I don't know what Linden was on about. Red's face wasn't a picture at all. He put his mobile back in his pocket, stood up and waved to us. Flavia obviously didn't have a clue what was going on and simply looked over in our direction. Dilly leapt to her feet and came running to meet us. 'Hi Maddy!' she called, as if we'd been friends for years. 'Wish I'd stayed on the beach with you. Flavia's been so boring. Wouldn't go *anywhere* in case Re—' she acknowledged Linden somewhat frostily – 'your brother showed up.'

'Don't blame me. I'm not his keeper,' said Linden and went ahead to join Red.

'Ugh,' said Dilly at Linden's departing back. 'She thinks she's so great, little Miss film-director's daughter. At least Red is *friendly*.' She laughed ruefully. 'That's the trouble. Even I know he's just being polite because he's got a nice personality, but Flavia's utterly convinced it's because he fancies her!'

Dad looked quite at home by the pool, well oiled, fat paperback and cold drink at his side – the burdens of caring for a teenage daughter can't have been weighing on him too heavily. Brian was obviously telling him things and Dad was nodding from time to time, probably, from what I know of him, not paying much attention. Gina Hayter unfolded herself from her sunbed as we approached. She might have a horsy face but she has a sinewy suntanned body, unlike poor old Flavia who has fair skin to go with the red hair and has to wear a sarong and filmy blouse for protection.

'What frightfully good timing,' said Gina. 'We were trying to persuade your father down to a beach bar for lunch. We're meeting Jonty down there. Look Richard,' she called. 'Your daughter's turned up right on cue!'

'So hunger finally brought you to heel did it?' Dad asked me.

Give me a break, Dad. 'Not true, Dad. I said I'd be here at lunch-time and here I am.'

'Ooh, beg pardon,' said Dad, smirking at Brian and Gina. I caught Red's eye in a 'parents, huh?' moment and had a sudden desire for the others to all disappear. What was he doing there, anyway?

'Well, it's super that you're here,' said Brian Hayter.

'Let's all go and have lunch together. I hope you and Linden will both come too, Redwood. I know Jonty wanted a word with you.'

Linden looked sulky, but Red actually said, 'Sure! Thank you, sir!' (Can you believe it?)

Gina said to the girls, 'Let's not bother to change,' (can you believe *that*? Why should they want to change?) and we set off back the way we'd come to a beach bar under the palms. Bliss.

Jonty was there already, perched on a bar stool in his boardies, sipping a long fruity drink through a straw. His hair was wet and his legs were sandy. His towel was in a heap at his feet. He looked happy.

'God, Jont, you're *disgusting!*' said Flavia before sitting on the stool furthest away from him. 'Banana daiquiri please Dad.'

Brian Hayter smiled jovially. 'Banana daiquiris for all the ladies then?'

Trust Dad to start. 'But they're alcoholic aren't they Brian?' I wasn't keen on him blabbing about my age right then, and I also fancied a straight fruit juice with loads of ice.

'Pineapple juice for me please,' I said quickly.

'BD for me,' said Dilly.

'G and T for me, darling,' said Gina, settling herself.

'And how about you two?' said Brian to Red and Linden. 'We're fine with fruit juice, sir, thanks,' said Redwood. He sat down with Jonty and Linden, so I joined them. Dilly hovered and came to rest by me, leaving the grown-ups to fill in the spaces between us and Flavia. Poor old Flavia had shot herself in the foot by dissociating herself from Jonty, because of course it was Jonty Red had been looking for all along.

'Hey, Red,' said Jonty. 'The windsurfing's ace, but here's the deal – if we go along later we can book into a trip to the east coast where the surf's more spectacular. I think we should check it out.'

'I already did,' said Red. 'Dad took me there a couple of years back, but if the club organises it that's cool. I'll come with you. What about you, Lin?'

'Maybe,' said Linden noncommittally.

'So have you all been here together before?' I asked.

'I was going to ask the same of you!' said Red. I had that smug feeling that he was trying to find a way of talking to me.

'I met Red windsurfing last year,' said Jonty. 'He's wicked at it. I'm just a beginner by comparison. And there was that other guy, Matt, from the hotel. He was the same age as me—'

'They were kinda like kid brothers,' said Red. 'But that was last year. You're catching up fast, man!' He threw a punch at Jonty.

'I wonder if Matt will show up this year?' said Jonty.

Linden joined in. 'I didn't like him much. I hope he doesn't.'

'That's only because he was better than you at everything,' said Red.

'No, not really. It was more because he wanted to be with you all the time and I felt left out. And I didn't like his Mom. It was all "poor old Matty-Matt – it's so nice for him to have *some*thing he's good at".'

Jonty laughed. ' "Poor old Matty-Matt" milked it for

all it was worth, didn't he? He was fine away from his mum, though. My sisters took against her, too. They said she didn't like *girls*, full stop – too much competition!'

Linden clearly bore a grudge. 'It was all the silly little things, like "Oh Linda, would you awfully mind if poor old Matty-Matt went on the banana boat instead of you this one time? It's just so nice for him to have Edward to be friends with." That was another thing, she insisted on calling us Linda and Edward. It used to make me mad. She just didn't care about anyone other than Matty-Matt.'

Dilly joined in with us now. 'He cheated at tennis. He always said it was out when we could *see* it was in! He had to win. And his mum said just that – "Poor old Matty-Matt! It's so nice for him to be good at tennis," as if the rest of his life was unbearable.'

'Probably was,' said Linden, 'with her for a mom!' Everybody laughed.

Brian brought us our drinks. 'Something seems to be amusing all of you,' he said as he handed them round.

'Just that boy Matt last year, Daddy,' said Dilly, 'and his awful mother. They were here for our first week. Do you remember?'

'Fine figure of a woman, if she's the one I'm thinking of,' said Brian. 'What was her name?'

'Who, darling?' Gina lit a cigarette and blew smoke rings.

'Matt's mum,' said Dilly.

'Oh!' said Gina, inhaling. 'Her!' She blew out more smoke, mostly through her nostrils. 'What *was* her name?'

Dad was in on this now. He smiled from Brian to Gina over his rum sour as they racked their brains.

'I know—' said Brian.

'It was—' said Gina –

'Fay!' they both said together. And for some reason the name made Dad splutter his drink all down his Hawaiian shirt.

'Mummy, are we going to eat, or what?' Flavia whined from her distant post.

'Oh yes,' said my dad. 'Food, food. What we all need is some food. Now, last year I became very partial to that barbecued fish. You should try it, Maddy.' So we all got on with ordering and eating our food. I could get used to this! I wanted to send an instant satellite video shot to Mum and Lo-lo, so they could share in the fun of being in this fabulous place by the blue, blue sea, in the cool shade of the palm trees, eating yummy food without caring how much it cost.

Food plus warmth makes me sleepy. Add to that a few hours of confused body clock and I suddenly felt I needed a siesta. I wanted to be somewhere dark and cool – like my room. 'Dad, do you mind if I go back to the hotel and have a bit of a rest?' I asked.

His face fell. 'I was looking forward to spending some time with you on the beach, sweetheart, or by the pool.'

'Not for long – just an hour or so. Anyway—' I suddenly realised the sun had gone in and clouds were piling up. 'It looks like rain!' That was surprising. Rain was the last thing I expected here. How wrong can you be?

'Oh, that's nothing,' he said. 'It'll all be over in ten minutes. But go on, darling. Have a rest if you need one. I'll come and get you in – what shall we say, one hour, two hours?'

'Make it two, Daddy. Gives me time for a shower as well.'

Red was suddenly at my side. 'I'll walk back with you, Maddy. I've got to pick up my stuff – thought I might bring the camcorder down.' Linden was talking to Jonty, and I got the feeling Red was hoping he could slip away without his sister noticing. He was being distinctly furtive.

We had only gone a short way when the first huge drops of rain began to fall. After all that heat it was blissful. 'Do you want to shelter?' Red asked, 'Or get wet?'

'Definitely get wet!' I told him.

'Let's go for it!' he shouted and pulled me into the middle of the tropical garden, turning his face up to the sky and holding out his arms. 'Woo-hoo!'

It was like a warm shower. I was soaked right through. Red put his arm through mine and we danced a silly little jig right there, and got a clap from some of the people sheltering under the trees. We gave them a bow.

The rain was easing up already. 'I feel as if I've known you a long time already,' said Red, 'but we haven't really had a chance to talk yet. Oh – and don't mind Lin.'

'What do you mean, "don't mind her"? I really like her.'

'Well, she comes on a bit strong sometimes, and she's a bit clingy round me – big brother, you know.'

'Well, I'm a big sister, so I do know.'

'She also, er, "expands" the truth sometimes. How can I say it? – just don't believe quite everything she says. It comes from being brought up in Tinseltown. We can't always tell the difference between reality and fantasy. Well, I like to think I can, but I'm not so sure about her. I don't want to be disloyal – we're real close – but I think I like you and I don't want you to be misled.'

'That's a very long speech from someone who looks half-drowned!'

'You don't look so great yourself! Actually – that's not the slightest bit true. You look fantastic – like some sort of mermaid.'

I blushed at the image. Not that I minded. He looked gorgeously hunky with his wet shirt clinging to his bronzed skin, and the rain making dark spots in his sunbleached hair. He shook himself like a dog before we went into the foyer. 'They don't like it if you're too casual here,' he said. 'Don't want us lowering the tone!'

'Maddy! You're all WET!' I knew that little voice. It was Bianca. She was in a swimsuit and her dad was carrying her. 'I'm going swimming, Maddy! Look – I've got armbands *and* a rubber ring!'

'Wow!' I said. 'Everybody had better get out of *your* way then!'

'Will you come swimming?' she asked.

'I'm just going for a rest, sweetheart,' I said. 'Perhaps by tomorrow we'll be in synch.'

'Don't worry, Maddy,' said her dad. He looked as sleepy as I felt.

'Tell you what, Bianca,' I'd had an idea. 'How about Mummy and Daddy having cocktails on their own tonight while I read you some bedtime stories? Would you like that?'

'Yes *please*!' said Bianca.

'Won't you be having cocktails of a sort yourself at that hour?' said her dad.

'Hardly!' I told him. 'But I know from my mum and my little sister that parents sometimes need a break from their children. And I like reading to Bianca – she reminds me of Eloise.'

'Well, that's very kind of you,' he said. 'Her bed-time's around 7.30.'

'See you then, Bianca!' I said. 'Have a good swim!'

I'd forgotten Red. 'What's the story there?' he asked. 'Why doesn't the kid have hair?'

I was already used to Bianca, but telling her story brought tears to my eyes. 'She's got leukaemia and she's dying,' I said. 'They've brought her here for a sort of perfect last family holiday. She's quite perky now, but she has to rest a lot. They're all so *brave*.'

'I think you need your rest,' said Red. 'You going to be around in the evening? Before your storytelling? I'm out on the water with Jonty this afternoon but how about we get together about six? Meet you at the beach bar?'

'I'm going to need a diary! But yes, fine. I imagine that's where everyone will be anyway, won't they?'

'As long as you're there, and I'm there, that's all I

care about! See you later!' and he disappeared off to their suite.

I tottered along to ours. Wow. Red wasn't slow in coming forward! It was nice though. I felt flattered. I pulled the curtains and stretched out on my cool bed – and knew no more.

I was woken by a tap on the door and Dad popped his head round. 'Time to wake up, Sleeping Beauty. I'm going to fix you a lovely cool drink with lots of ice while you get up, have a shower or whatever. See you in ten minutes.'

'Mmmmm. Thanks Dad.' I struggled into conscious-ness.

I had a shower, dressed in dry clothes over a dry bikini and went to join Dad. He handed me my drink. 'What do you want to do now, darling?'

'I can't believe we've been here less than twenty-four hours. I feel I've done all sorts of things, met all sorts of people. It's incredible how much can happen in a short time isn't it? All I want to do for the rest of today is sit around, by the pool or on the beach I suppose. Have you any idea what the other kids are doing?'

'The Hayter girls went somewhere to find horses, I know that. And young Jonty went off with Red, closely followed by Red's sister. *Are* there any more?'

'On the beach this morning there were loads. A whole cricket team from Beale College in London – plus their families. There was a girl called Holly who was really nice. Still, I expect they're playing cricket!'

'Shall we just go down to the pool or the beach,

then? Take something to read? I expect Brian and Gina are down by the pool. There's plenty of time for excursions.'

'A whole two weeks! This is so brilliant, Dad. Thank you for taking a whole two weeks out of your busy schedule to spend just with little me.' I gave him a hug.

Dad hugged me back. 'Well,' he said. 'Everyone needs a holiday.'

'You don't seem to have met up with anyone you know yet, though.'

'Oh. No. Well. I expect some of them will turn up next week.'

'Any cool teenagers amongst them?'

'No,' he said quickly. 'Not this time. Huh. Well, we'll see won't we?'

'Some of the teenagers here already are quite cool. Well, one of them, anyway!' I laughed. I didn't mind Dad knowing I liked Red.

'If you're talking about Red, I noticed that he couldn't keep his eyes off you! Now, go easy, young lady.'

'Not my fault, Dad!'

'He seems a pleasant enough lad.'

'Not much competition so far. Unless you count the entire cricket team! And Red's dad, of course. He's pretty cool for an old guy.'

'A bit less of the old, thank you very much. He's only in his early forties – like I am.'

'I said he was cool.'

'Like me?'

I humoured him. 'Like you, Dad.'

*

Dad and I had a really nice companionable time down on the beach under a sun umbrella. You'd burn in ten minutes in the full sun. He read his paperback. I had *West Side Story* with me, but I didn't look at it much. I watched the Hobie Cats and the water-skiers and the banana boats out in the bay, though I was feeling far too slothful to want to go on anything right now. When either of us got too hot we went and cooled down in the sea. What a life! Red's dad and entourage were a little way off and I enjoyed watching them too. Oliver seemed to spend most of his time on the mobile. Obviously a workaholic. I remembered Linden's advice to steer clear of him – and then Red's warnings about Linden's attitude towards the truth. And then I saw a troop of boys and Holly running into the sea further down the beach and forgot about the O'Neills altogether.

'That's the cricket team, Dad,' I said, and pointed in their direction. 'I'm just going over to say hello to Holly. Back in a mo!' I ran over and called to Holly.

Holly waved. 'Hi Maddy!' I caught up with her. 'The boys have just lost their match, so they're taking out their frustrations on the waves. And cooling down. It's really hot for them when they're playing. What have you been doing this afternoon?'

'Sleeping, mostly,' I said.

'What about Linden?'

'She went off with Jonty and her brother – wind-surfing again I think.'

'Have you met her brother, Red? He looks like a film star.'

'Well, I suppose he is from Hollywood! Yes, I've met him. He seems a really nice guy. I'm meeting him at the beach bar soon.'

'Really? Lucky thing! Though I'm not surprised, looking like you do. I suppose he's not much older than us – sixteen or so?'

'It's hard to tell, isn't it? I can't work out how old Linden is either.'

'Oh she's fourteen, like us. I assume you're fourteen too?'

Girls your own age are the hardest ones to lie to about such matters. 'I'm fifteen next month,' I told her. 'But no one ever questions my fake ID!'

'OK,' she said. 'So if Charles or anyone asks, you're over sixteen?'

'Why not!' I said, and we both laughed. 'Where do you live? Beale College isn't that far from my house.' It turns out that she goes to a state school similar to mine. In fact our lads play them at football (but not cricket!). It's like having Hannah or Sophie here to stop me getting too carried away by all the high life.

'I've got to go,' she said. 'It's time to go back for supper with the boys. See you on the beach tomorrow morning perhaps?'

'Probably,' I said, and then saw that it was already six o'clock. 'I must dash off too – got a boy to meet in a bar.'

'Lucky cow!' Holly is *my* sort of friend.

I ran back to Dad. Brian Hayter had found him and they were discussing golf. Yawn. I grabbed my towel and my script. 'Dad, I said I'd meet Red at six – See you later?'

'What – yes – sorry Brian – fine. So, see you for supper, Maddy?'

'Yup.'

I walked over to the beach bar. The first person I saw was Linden. Then Jonty. Red was buying drinks. He kept looking round – I suppose he was looking for me. 'I fancy a plain old coke, please,' I said ducking round him.

'Maddy! You're here.' His eyes lit up, gratifyingly. 'Good. Sure. Another Coke please. Too bad about the others being here – you were right.'

Linden and Jonty were both pleased to see me – I don't think they have much in common. I found myself looking at Linden slightly differently, which was a shame, because I want to like her. I *do* like her! She told me all about the windsurfing and how I should give it a try.

'It's brilliant,' said Jonty. 'Everyone should give it a try. You teach her, Red!'

'I'm only qualified to teach scuba diving. Beginners need proper grown-up instructors,' said Red. 'But it's all part of the hotel programme.'

'Perhaps Dilly would do it with me?' I asked Jonty.

'If Flavia will let her go. I'll ask her if you like.'

Red sat down next to me. I saw that he was left-handed, which meant that his drinking arm rested beside mine, and every now and then the hairs on it brushed against my skin as he raised his glass or set it down. I pretended not to notice – I didn't think he was doing it on purpose, but you can never quite tell . . . It was nice, anyway – I wasn't going to move. I hardly got to speak to him though, because as soon as he sat down, Jonty demanded all his attention and Linden demanded all of mine.

'I'm sure you'd be good at windsurfing – and the other watersports. It's what our hotel's best for. Do you do any other sports? You look kinda fit.'

'I do a lot of dance-drama stuff and singing, so I have to be fit – and quick at learning, physically. I just haven't had the opportunities to do any of these water things. We usually bunk off games and gym at school. Girls' football isn't my idea of fun!'

'I guess I can imagine you doing all that dance stuff. You've got the right kind of figure. And you're pretty. Maybe you should talk to my father! NO! Don't even think about it. You know what I said before.'

'What are you telling Maddy about Dad, Linden?' Red was in there, quick as a flash.

'Only joking, Red. Guess what! Maddy's learning *West Side Story* for her school production!'

'Hey!' said Red, 'Did you know my father's doing a film version with young teenage stars – kinda like Zeffirelli's *Romeo and Juliet*?'

'Linden told me,' I said carefully. 'A school production's quite a big enough challenge for me!'

The sun was setting. It happens suddenly here – very dramatic. 'Check out that sunset!' said Red, *West Side Story* forgotten, thank goodness. 'Guys – I want to video that.' He reached down for the camcorder. 'Take your drinks down to the water – I'll shoot you all there. Go on, take off your sandals and leap about in the water – make some good silhouettes for me.' We did as we were told.

'Let's tango!' said Jonty – surprisingly, and swept me into a smart bit of Latin dancing. Well, I can just about do it, but *Jonty*! He led with all the turns and the straight arm movements down to a tee. He was really good! Especially considering we were dancing in the sea!

'Where did you learn that, Jonty?'

'Oh, my parents don't pay astronomical school fees for nothing, you know. *Turn*. We get to do ballroom dancing with the girls school down the road once a week in year nine. *Head swivel*. And if a thing's worth doing, it's worth doing well – as Dad always says. *Lean together*. Actually, Mum and Dad made us all have lessons in the hols too – Flavia's ball is in the spring. *And again.*'

'I don't know what ya talking about, Jonty,' said Linden. 'But I'm impressed by the fancy footwork! And you, Maddy! You know they have a dance here in the hotel once a week. Not that anyone under twenty-five would be seen dead there!'

Red was scampering about with his camcorder. 'That was totally outta this world! Who'd a thought I could have found two kids to tango against the sunset for me. Wow! Not even Dad could manage that!'

'JONTY! Jonty! JONATHAN!' It was Flavia. 'Mother says to come and change for dinner. What *are* you doing?'

'Can you dance, too, Flavia?' Red asked. Flavia blushed like the sunset.

'Are you asking?' she said, looking down, coyly.

'Well, no, not exactly!' I could see Red wondering what he'd got himself into. 'We're just all so stunned by Jonty's prowess on the dance floor – especially as it's just the beach.'

'Well, we go to balls, you see,' said Flavia. As if that explained it. 'And though they're usually just a scrum, it pays to know what one's doing. Especially at our local hunt bash. And I'm having mine in the spring.'

So Flavia's a deb! I've never met a deb before. She realised that this wasn't an invitation from Red and quickly recovered herself. 'Do come on, Jonty. The parents are waiting.'

I looked at my watch. It was seven-fifteen. 'I'll have to come up with you,' I said. I looked apologetically at Red. 'Bianca! See you later, maybe!' and ran after Flavia who was marching ahead with Jonty hopping along to keep up with her.

Bianca was all tucked up in bed surrounded by soft toys. There were some the hotel had donated as well as all the ones she could carry on the plane. On a shelf near her bed was a vast array of bottles and pots of pills and potions. Poor little mite. She looked pale and drained, but pleased to see me.

'She's had all her medication,' said her mum. 'We're very grateful, Maddy. The hotel does have a babysitting service, but we don't really want to leave her with strangers. And she likes you so much – don't you darling? Here's our mobile number. We'll be back in forty-five minutes, but call us if there's a problem.

We're not far away!' They went off and I sat on Bianca's bed.

'I've chosen my stories,' she said. 'They're all cheerful ones because I've been sad this evening.'

'Oh, Bianca,' I said. 'You don't want to be sad, not here.'

'I'm sad when Mummy and Daddy are sad. They're sad about me dying.'

'Bianca!' What on *earth* do you say in this situation?

'I don't mind dying. I love God, and I really want to meet Him, you see. But I love Mummy and Daddy, too.'

'And I love you, too, Bianca, because you remind me of my little sister, so I want to read you a lovely happy story to make you smile. What have you got for me? Ooh – *Winnie the Pooh*, that's nice.'

'Tigger's happy!'

'And *The Cat in the Hat*.'

'The cat makes me laugh. And one more . . .'

I thought three stories was about right. 'Have you got *The Snowman*? – that's Eloise's favourite. Only it's not very seasonal!'

'Of course I've got *The Snowman*. I think I might be able to walk on the air one day. Are you really going to read me three stories?'

'Yup. Are you sitting comfortably?' Kids! They wrench you one way and then the other – but I really wasn't prepared for the emotions that Bianca brought out in me. She fell asleep with a smile on her face when I finished *The Snowman*, but I was feeling pretty weepy by then. Read it for yourself and you'll see why. I splashed cold water on my face and dried it just before I heard the key in the lock.

'Perfect timing!' I whispered as they came in. 'She's just dropped off.'

'Was she OK?' asked her mum. 'She's had a lot of pain today.'

'Poor little scrap,' said her dad. 'But you know kids, they're so resilient, so brave. She ends up trying to cheer *us* up.'

'She chose cheerful stories for me to read.'

'Well, thanks. It was lovely to have a break.'

'I'm really happy to read to her most nights. And, another thing. Might she be able to cope with a banana boat ride if I hung on to her? I went on one this morning, and I thought how much Bianca would love it.'

'I don't know,' said her dad. 'Maybe on a good day. You might have to strap her to you, literally. But let's see. I wouldn't rule it out.'

'I'd better go.' I looked at my watch. It was already half-past eight. I hoped Dad would wait for me before eating.

Five

I woke up feeling that I had been here for ever. Dad and I both emerged from our rooms, showered and ready for action, at about the same time. He outlined our schedule for the day (has to have it all planned out, my dad) as we walked through the tropical gardens to breakfast. 'On Dilly's advice I booked you in for the watersports this afternoon. It's a scuba diving lesson if you want one. Some of the other kids are doing it, too. I might have a go myself one day – I never got round to it last year – but not today because I'm playing golf with Brian Hayter. Gina and Flavia will be out riding, I gather.'

We loaded our plates with luscious fruit – slices of mango and pineapple and papaya. 'And tonight there's something rather naff that Gina describes as "very touristy but frightful fun". They hold a beach barbecue at one of the hotels further round the bay. Steel band, limbo dancing for all-comers, good barbecue. Has to be done, I reckon, don't you?'

'We *are* tourists. I don't mind. I think it sounds cool. Will the others come?'

'Where you go, sweetheart, I'm sure others will follow. I don't know, but let's ask them.'

I spent the morning by the pool. Bianca was down there. She was having a good day. I towed her around the children's pool for ages and she was dead bossy – just like Lo-lo. Dilly and Jonty turned up around lunch-time. They wanted to know if I was coming on the watersports course. 'And we're all going limbo dancing tonight,' said Jonty. 'Every year the parents pretend that it's far too common for us, but they absolutely love it.'

'It's Mum, mostly – there's this enormous guy in a grass skirt who helps you under the bar and we reckon Mum has the hots for him. She always goes back for more,' said Dilly. 'And guess what – Charles and the Beale College lot are all coming too. Holly told me.'

'Charles *and* the Beale College lot . . .' Jonty started mincing around. Dilly smacked him round the head. I'm glad I don't have brothers.

'Flavia's desperate for Red to come with us, so I suppose that means Linden too. Do you think we can persuade them?'

'I think Maddy could probably persuade Red to do most things,' said Jonty. I know he's not *my* brother, but I took the liberty of smacking him round the head *à la* Dilly.

'We'll see them this afternoon, won't we?' I said. 'Who exactly is doing what, watersportswise?'

'Jonty and I are both doing the scuba diving. I've got a feeling Linden might be too. She was keen when we were talking about it last night. So with you as well we can be two pairs.'

'Red doesn't need lessons, he's got an instructor's certificate already,' said Jonty. 'He dives with a camera – he's really interested in all that sea life stuff. I expect Linden's quite experienced too, though she might be like us – just the odd holiday lesson now and then that doesn't really add up to anything serious.'

At lunch Dad was all kitted out for golf. Not a pretty sight. Dilly and I set off for the beach together. We stood watching some people parascending – it looked completely brilliant, but quite scary, especially with all those maniac jetskiers zipping about. One of the jetskiers came back to the beach. It was Red. He saw us as he was beaching the jetski, and came over. 'Maddy! Hi! What are you two waiting for?'

'Scuba diving,' I told him.

'Linden's coming down for that too,' he said. 'You'll love it. There's so much to look at down there. I do it a lot.' He pointed out into the bay. 'That's your boat, so you won't have long to wait.'

Dilly had been waiting for him to draw breath before butting in. 'Red – might you and Linden be coming to the beach barbecue thing tonight? Maddy's coming, aren't you Maddy?'

'Sure,' said Red, 'if it's open to anyone. When are you leaving?' he asked me.

'I don't know,' I said, 'but why don't we meet at the beach bar at six again?'

Jonty chose that moment to join us. 'Secret assignation or can we all come?'

'It's just so we can meet up with Red and Linden before going out tonight,' said Dilly.

'Huh! So you've been persuaded to join the limbo dancing team, have you?' he said to Red.

'No one mentioned limbo dancing!' said Red. 'But now I can't wait!' Linden was running towards us. 'Hi, Lin. You having a refresher course then?'

'Sure am,' said Linden. 'Hey, Red, take my mobile would you? I don't want it to get wet.' She threw it to him as our instructor came towards us, and Red set off up the beach to the hotel.

Linden, Jonty and Dilly were all very laid back about our scuba diving lesson – they'd done it before. I might skip gym at school, but I'm a good swimmer. Swimming was one of the things Dad and I used to do when he still lived with us, and it was also one of the things we used to do on Sundays when he took me out. Our instructor was gorgeous. He made me feel very safe as he checked out our swimming and diving experience. We wore our swimsuits – no need for wetsuits in this warm water. He told us a bit about scuba diving first – I mean, did *you* know that SCUBA stands for Self-Contained Underwater Breathing Apparatus? Because I didn't! You have to do it in pairs, for safety, and you have signals that you make to each other about coming up, going down, and so on. I found I was concentrating very hard.

And then, we were off. We wore our oxygen packs on our backs and carried our flippers and goggles to walk out to the boat. We sailed out into the bay where the coral is, and then flippers, goggles and noseclips on – check breathing apparatus, and backwards over the side of the boat we went. I was paired with Linden. She certainly wouldn't have let me go with either of the others – but it was good because she knew what to do. It was FANTASTIC. It was like being in a completely different world. I felt transformed into a bubble-blowing sea creature, flitting about over the coral reef, part of an enormous and wonderfully choreographed water ballet – I practically had the soundtrack going through my brain.

There was a nasty moment when I was following

Linden closely and looked around to see that we had lost the other two. I had a feeling our time was up and I tried to use my signals, but Linden didn't take any notice. In the end I propelled myself into her, working my flippers overtime, and grabbed her. She turned round, then, and we were back with the others quite quickly, and making for the surface. I could tell when we came up that we had worried the instructor, and he had a bit of a go at us. Linden pretended not to care, but I could see she was rattled. I tried to apologise without making it obvious that it had been Linden's fault, but I think he knew.

Overall it had been wonderful. I couldn't wait to do it again. A little thought crept into my mind that it would be fabulous to dive with Red. I stored it for the time being. Meanwhile the others were comparing notes on all they had seen. 'We need Red here,' said Linden, as if she's read my mind. 'He's brilliant on all this stuff. He knows the names of everything on the reef.'

I felt as if we'd been out for ages but it was only mid-afternoon. We stopped off at the beach bar for a drink. 'Where did you two go down there?' Dilly asked. 'I didn't think it would be possible to lose anyone in that short time.'

'Probably Linden showing off, eh?' Jonty seemed to feel he could treat Linden as an honorary sister too.

'Just enjoying myself,' said Linden. 'I thought you guys could look after yourselves.'

'So what about Maddy?' said Dilly, aggrieved on my behalf. 'Bet you gave her a fright.'

'Maddy's cool,' said Linden. 'She didn't mind – did you Maddy?'

I decided to laugh this one off. 'So what does everybody want to drink then?'

I chose to go back to my room for a bit. I wanted to flop around and then have a shower and the chance to do my make-up properly before we met up with Red again. The more time I spent away from him the more I looked forward to seeing him. I liked being with Linden because she was a connection, but there were things about Linden that were difficult. It was as if she *owned* her brother. I almost felt I had to stay in with her, because if she didn't like me she would certainly make it difficult to be with Red. And she was picky about the people she spent time with. Her father certainly wasn't one of them. And she didn't have much time for Dilly. She seemed comfortable with the cricketers – perhaps they were a good audience. Oooh, Maddy. Mentally I slapped my own wrist. It wouldn't do to start having bitchy thoughts about Linden.

I washed my hair in the shower and tried out the lovely aloe vera conditioner. Great believers in aloe vera the Barbadians, it seems to me. They sell a gorgeous cool aloe vera sunscreen on the beach as well. I put on a green top and a short white skirt – I hoped I wouldn't have to change again for the barbecue. I couldn't tell if the Hayters would turn up wearing ballgowns.

I checked myself out in the mirror. The tan is coming along nicely and my hair is starting to streak.

I had a tweak at the eyebrows – thinner eyebrows show off my eyelashes. They're so long they're sometimes a bit of a nuisance. I put on some foundation. The colour looked a bit at odds with my tan, but it covered up everything else, including a couple of spots I could see starting on my forehead. I blended two lots of eyeshadow, brown and gold and then some very dark brown eyeliner and black mascara. I know you're not supposed to use black if you're a blonde, but since my eyelashes are black anyway I think it's OK. Then I found some blusher and put it on to make my cheekbones stand out. I sat back to admire the overall effect.

Aagh. No. Too much! I was only meeting the others for a drink. They might have just come out of the water. I grabbed the tissues and started to wipe it all off. When one half was wiped and the other was horribly over made-up the phone rang. Who would ring us? I went into our living room and picked it up. It was Linden on her mobile. 'Where are you, Maddy? It's six o'clock and everyone else is here, including your dad.' I hadn't realised it was that late.

'I'll be right over.' Help. I wiped all the make-up off, whacked on some lip gloss and squirted myself with the Hugo Boss. I was even beginning to feel nervous – and I liked it! ROMANCE! Red, here I come . . .

The barbecue starts quite early because it's a family do. We were going to walk along the beach. 'Is your dad coming?' I asked the O'Neills.

'No way!' said Linden, laughing scornfully. 'You won't find him mixing with the masses!'

Flavia looked offended. I could see she wanted to say that this wasn't the sort of thing they usually went to, but Red said, 'He's so lazy! If he doesn't need to set foot outside his hotel on holiday, then he won't! I've got the camcorder though – I'll be able to show him what he's missing!' He looked at me and Jonty. 'You two started it. I've decided to shoot as many sorts of dancing as I can. Dad approves. He's into dancing right now because of *West Side Story*.'

'What's all this? What have you and Jonty been getting up to now, Maddy?' said Dad, smiling indulgently. He clearly approved of my friendship with Jonty, us being the same age (not that Jonty knows) and everything.

'Oh, just a spot of tangoing on the beach,' said Jonty, enjoying himself.

Flavia said, 'Oh, Jonty! Why do you always have to be so em*bar*rassing?' She looked pained at the memory of Jonty shaming her family in front of Red.

Dad still looked puzzled. 'Jonty's ace at Latin dancing, Dad. Life is full of surprises, isn't it?' Jonty got up and did a twirl just as Brian and Gina Hayter appeared. Gina was wearing *slacks* (for limbo dancing, no doubt), I noticed, and a lot of make-up.

'Gina would insist on the dancing classes,' said Brian gruffly. 'But the boy does himself proud on the rugby field too.'

'So that's OK then,' said Dilly mischievously. 'Come on! The Beale College lot are getting there at six-thirty, Holly said so. And it will be so much more fun if we're all there together.'

We kicked off our shoes and walked along the beach to a hotel less than a mile away. I could see Red manoeuvring himself into position alongside me. For once Linden was more than a few metres away, talking about Charles from Beale College with Dilly. 'So how was the scuba diving?' Red asked as he fell in beside me. 'I've already heard about Linden being irresponsible from the instructor. She does actually know what she's doing and you weren't in any real danger, but I had a go at her myself. I told her I wouldn't tell Dad – he'd forbid her from going again and there'd be a helluva row – but I thought I might come along and go down with you next time. Did you like the fish? Did you see any angel fish?'

'It was brilliant,' I said. 'But I couldn't tell you what I did and didn't see. I can't tell fishy things apart.'

'You definitely need me then,' he told me, and smiled to himself when he realised what he'd just said. He looked down at me, to see if I'd realised too, as we walked along the edge of the sea in the evening light. A warm breeze ruffled his hair and the low sun cast long shadows of his striding figure. He looked like a Hollywood Viking – but Red was no actor: the warmth in his blue eyes was one hundred per cent real.

The barbecue was fun. We queued for our food and sat down at long tables on the beach. Red sat next to me and was very attentive. Flavia didn't like it, neither did Linden, but I decided that that was their problem. I liked it a lot. Not being alone meant that we talked about general things all the time, when really I wanted to get to know him better, but I reckoned there would be time for all that over the next two weeks. Holly came over to us and pointed out where their enormous party was sitting. We agreed to meet up for the limbo dancing. I could see Dilly peering over in their direction trying to pick out smarmy Charles. She kept pulling out a make-up bag and retouching her lipstick in the mirror.

A steel band had been playing all along, but now the music was louder and a guy with a lovely deep voice told us over the p.a. that the limbo dancing competition was about to begin. Gina was one of the first to get up and go over to him. She even stubbed her cigarette out and put the holder away in her handbag. It shouldn't have been a surprise that she and Brian were good dancers, considering Jonty, but boy, did she love shimmying under the bar. I could see why. It was a real challenge – and for a few brief moments all eyes were on each competitor. Red's camcorder was on us too.

The first few rounds took ages. There were about a hundred people at the barbecue and at least fifty wanted a go at limbo dancing – in between jigging around to the steel band. It was a shame Red was videoing all the time, or we might have had a dance. Still, Jonty and the entire cricket team were willing partners. So, more embarrassingly, were Brian Hayter and Dad. The bar was getting lower. I knocked it off and went to stand by Red for a bit. 'Are you filming everyone as they go under?'

'No! I only press the button when I think it's interesting. But I don't want people to know when I'm focusing on them. Like you, for instance!'

'Red!'

'You're such a cool dancer! Over there too. It's a good job I have to take my eyes off you to film this!' Gina was going under the bar. She was pretty good. Stomach muscles like steel. She went back to where Dad was standing with Brian. As I watched, another couple came over and greeted them. They seemed to know Dad too.

'Were those people who are talking to my dad and the Hayters here last year, Red?' I asked him.

He turned the camcorder in their direction. 'Yes – at our hotel. They must be staying somewhere different this year.'

'I wonder what they're saying to Dad.'

'I'll zoom in on them if you like, and see if I can lip read. In fact, how about you try?'

'OK.' He showed me how to use it, taking the opportunity to push my hair off my face so I could look into it properly. Again I wanted all those people to disappear. But instead I focused on Dad and his cronies. The new couple greeted him fulsomely.

I didn't need to lip read – the woman had a booming voice. 'Richard!' she said. 'Are you here on your own, then?' At which point I would have expected Dad to shake his head and nod in my direction. But he didn't. He did look up and see me pointing a camcorder at him though, and turned his back on me. Then I heard a name I'd heard before: 'When's Fay arriving?' asked the woman, but I didn't hear Dad's answer because he was facing away from me.

'Curious,' I said, shaken for some reason, as I handed back the camcorder to Red.

'Why?'

'They were talking about Fay. Isn't that the infamous mother of Matty-Matt?'

'Yes. I think Meryl and Fay were at the hotel when we were last year, though your dad must have left before we arrived.'

'I realise that. I just had a horrible thought that maybe Dad didn't come here just for my sake. You know how you end up spying on your parents.'

'I've given up doing that with my Dad, though Linden still watches him like a hawk. Forget it. I'm bored with the camcorder. Let's dance.'

So I danced with Red and forgot about Dad. It was very hot on the dance floor and the adults were all pretty drunk. We were all thrown together and it was brilliant. It wasn't couple dancing but Red grabbed me whenever I got pushed too far away. He had to lean close to make himself heard, and what with one thing and another we managed to find plenty of occasions for touching and bumping into each other. Every now and then I felt Flavia's or Linden's jealous eyes on me, though Linden was mostly busy with the cricket team and – apparently – enticing Charles away from poor old Dilly. Jonty seemed to be getting on very well with Holly. Only three days into the holiday and it was beginning to feel like one big happy family . . .

The family part of the barbecue was definitely over. The cricket team were led away and Flavia started rounding up Dilly (who was looking tearful) and Jonty (who was gazing longingly after the departing Holly). 'JONTY! Come ON!' said Flavia, cuffing him. 'You're FAR too young to be interested in girls. HONESTLY!' Meanwhile Gina had Dad transfixed with a smoke-ringed gaze from which he couldn't escape. Linden, having ruined Dilly's evening, now took it upon herself to comfort her, so Red and I were left to bring up the rear as we all walked back along the beach. We fell behind the others *almost* without realising it.

When they were safely out of sight around the curve of the bay Red stopped for a moment and leaned against a palm tree. The waves swished against the shore and the moon made a path over the sea. It was too romantic for words. 'Come here, Maddy,' he said, and held out both his hands to me. I moved towards him – and then two things happened simultaneously. His mobile rang and Dad came storming back to find us.

'Yes, Linden, I'm on my way,' said Red into his mobile, as Dad roared, 'Madeleine! I thought I'd lost you. Now stop loitering and come along at once!'

Six

I barely spoke to Dad on the way back to the hotel. Red was all apologetic – 'I'm sorry sir – we weren't far behind,' etc, etc. Dad had nodded grimly but practically dragged me back to our rooms, saying, 'Yes, well, it's late anyway.' When we got in I had a go at him, briefly, for behaving like the thought police, and couldn't I even have a bit of a holiday romance, or wasn't it *allowed*? It wasn't as if Red and I were even *doing* anything!

All he could say was that I was only fourteen and Red was seventeen and we didn't know him. I said I knew Red as well as he knew Brian Hayter, but that didn't stop *them* going off together, did it? I also reminded him that I was only a few weeks off fifteen and Red was only just seventeen. Then I detected Linden's hand in the affair because it all became a little clearer when Dad went on about us not knowing what *sort* of boy Red was. 'What do you mean, what *sort* of boy?' I asked him.

'Well, according to his sister, he's something of a . . .'

'Go on,' I said wearily, knowing that Linden would have deliberately put a spanner in the works.

' "Sex maniac" was the expression she used.'

'And you'd trust her judgement over mine?'

'I'm only trying to protect you, darling.'

'What from, exactly?'

'Oh, you know—'

'No I don't!' I yelled. 'You just don't want me to have any fun! You bring me on this brilliant holiday, expect me to look pretty and be grateful, but you just can't cope with a living, breathing teenage daughter. Look at me Dad! I am a teenage girl! I happen to like teenage boys! It's *normal*!'

Dad looked at me. Sadly, 'I'm sorry sweetheart. Give your silly old dad a hug.' I gave him a quick squeeze. I don't like hurting his feelings. 'I don't want to spoil your fun, Mads, I really don't. It's just that you're very young still.'

'Not that young, Dad. I watch television. I see movies. I hear the news. I go to a whacking great comprehensive school. You can't really protect me from the real world.'

'And that's what saddens me,' he said, pouring himself a drink and turning away.

'I'm off to bed now,' I said. 'See you in the morning, Daddy. Love you.'

'Love you too,' he said.

I woke up feeling cross. I'd forgiven Dad for last night in some ways, but he *had* interrupted me and Red. We'd been working up to that kiss all evening, and now I felt cheated. I tried to relive the moments just before. The anticipation had been delicious. I would just have to imagine the rest. Bother Linden! She's really good company, but I don't think I should trust her farther than I can throw her.

I thought about the day ahead. There was some beginners' windsurfing on the afternoon watersports schedule. Dilly said she'd do it with me – there's no way Jonty and Linden can be classed as beginners! And before that, some serious sunbathing on the beach. I might see Holly and the cricketers there – I like them, they remind me of home. And of course I want to catch up with Red, too, but somehow I don't want to plan that – I just want it to *happen*. And then there's Bianca. When did my social life get to be so busy?

Dad and I went down to breakfast together. He seemed almost sheepish. 'I hardly like to say this after your comments last night,' he said, 'but Brian has asked me to drive over to a new 18-hole golf course with him this afternoon. Would you mind being left here?'

'But Dad,' I teased, 'we hardly even *know* the man! Are you sure you should be leaving me? After all, I'm only fourteen . . .'

'Good gracious, child, you're nearly fifteen!'

'When it suits *you*, yes. But who'll look after me if I hurt myself windsurfing?'

Dad looked serious. 'Oh dear. You know I hadn't really considered that. Perhaps I'd better ask Gina. I'm a pretty hopeless father, aren't I?'

'Shut up, Dad. I'm just making you suffer for last night. I'm not really likely to hurt myself – unless that sex maniac Red catches up with me, of course!'

'I'll be back in time for supper.'

'You'd better be!'

It was still early and the cricketers were playing cricket on the beach while it was more or less empty. Holly and Abby came running over as soon as they saw me. '*You* looked as though you were having a nice time last night!' said Holly.

'So did *you*,' I said. 'Jonty and Dilly are on their way down now, even as we speak . . .'

'What are you talking about?' asked Abby, who

hadn't been to the barbecue. 'No one will tell me anything!'

Holly caught my eye and put her finger to her lips. 'It was a good barbecue,' I told Abby. 'We all really enjoyed the food.' Holly smiled gratefully, but then Jonty arrived and she started to blush.

'Hi,' said Jonty, at a loss for words – for the first time in his life I imagine.

'Hi,' said Holly.

No prizes for scintillating conversation there.

Then Dilly caught up with them, running in the heat, her feet sinking into the sand. She sat down in the shade of a beach umbrella to draw breath. 'Jont, Mum says you must come riding with us this morning if you want to go surfing on the east coast tomorrow. Don't ask me why. I think she must miss you or something. And the O'Neills are all off somewhere this morning too – Bridgetown I think – so you won't miss out on Red. Though *you* will, Maddy!' She turned to me. 'I don't know what makes Linden tick. She wasn't content just with getting Charles away from me, she had to ruin your evening, too. I heard her freaking out your dad by telling him that her brother was a bit of a sex maniac! Red of all people! He's such a gentleman!'

'Ooh, what's all this?' asked Holly, her eyes nearly as wide as Abby's.

'Get Maddy to tell you,' said Jonty. 'I have to go I'm afraid – see you later,' and he suddenly darted forward and gave Holly a peck on the cheek before heading back for the hotel with Dilly.

'*Lots* to talk about,' I said, as Holly put her hand up to touch her cheek where Jonty had kissed her, and we made ourselves very comfortable indeed on the sun-beds.

'Run away, Abby,' said Holly, not unkindly.

'Why can't I stay?'

'Big girls' talk. Now, go and find someone to play with – see if Mum's around.' With Abby dispatched, Holly settled in. I told her about my row with Dad. 'Trust Linden,' she said. 'Sometimes I think she's in love with her own brother! As for dads – mine throws a fit whenever he comes across one of my magazines. They seem to think that if we know what sex *is* we're going to run off and get pregnant – just like that! As if we mightn't be just a *teensy* bit choosy about who we do it with, or when? They never give us any credit do they?'

Dad came to say goodbye before he went off with Brian Hayter in search of the new golf course. Brian told me that Dilly would be back in time for the windsurfing and then they went off like two eager schoolboys and left me to have lunch on my own.

Dilly said I took to windsurfing like a duck to water, which seemed quite appropriate really. It was *brilliant* – I only fell in once. It's all a matter of balance – and I'm good at that. The sun was burning down – we really had to slap on the sunscreen before going out – but the sea and the breeze were cool. The instructor was very complimentary as well. It might just have been because he fancied me, but I'm much stronger (from all the dancing) than I look, so I think I surprised him. Oh dear – it's yet another thing I'm longing to do with Red. Now I know why he and Jonty love it so much – you just feel so free out there, you, the sea and the wind. Dilly says it's a bit like riding in a way, you're independent and in control, just you and the elements. What all teenagers need, with parents like ours!

As we walked back up the beach afterwards I saw a group of people waving to me from the deep shade of some palm trees. 'Come and meet Bianca!' I told Dilly. 'She must be feeling good today if they've brought her to the beach!'

'Maddy!' squealed Bianca. 'Mummy says I can go on a banana boat with you and Daddy. I've been waiting *hours* for you to finish your lesson!' Imperious little madam. I looked at her dad.

'We've devised a sort of harness for her – so you can strap her to the front of your lifejacket. She'll be pushed backwards by the thrust of the boat anyway. I'll sit in front as well, so if we go over we three will go together. What do you think?'

'He's thought of nothing else since you first mentioned it,' said Bianca's mum. 'And she's so *desperate* to have a go – we decided it was worth a try.'

'Fine by me,' I said. 'And if Dilly – this is my friend Cordelia Hayter – comes too we can have one to ourselves.'

'I would go,' said Bianca's mum, 'But it scares the life out of me just watching! I've never been much of a swimmer.'

'Come *on*!' said Bianca. So off we went to find a banana boat. The boat hire guy found a special small lifejacket for Bianca and we strapped her on to my front with a modified set of child's reins. The little thing was positively *trembling* with excitement as we were pulled into the bay. The boatman was brilliant – and went in wide curves so we didn't fall in, but then Bianca kept saying, 'I want to do it properly!' so I made a decision. Usually someone sets a banana boat undulating like a snake to make it even harder to stay on. When the trip was nearly over I bounced up and down once or twice and then rolled off into the sea, taking Bianca with me. I'd towed her around the pool enough – I felt pretty sure I knew what she was capable of. And she *loved* it – she just bobbed about with me, yelling '*Look at me! Look at me!*' I wasn't even out of my depth, so I unhitched her and towed her along, just like in the pool.

'You had me worried there,' said her dad, when we were back sitting on the beach.

'Me too,' said her mum. 'I was convinced she was going to drown.'

'I *loved* it!' said Bianca. 'It's the best thing I've ever done in my *whole* life!'

'That's why you did it, isn't it?' said Cordelia when we were in the beach bar later.

'Yup,' I said. 'She was *desperate* for the real thing. Wouldn't you be if you didn't have long to live?' I felt the tears pricking still at what Bianca had said. 'Her parents treat her like porcelain and it's not what she wants.'

'They have to do what they think is right though, don't they?' said Dilly.

'I suppose that's the thing with parents,' I said, thinking of Dad.

Dilly and I wandered back up to the hotel. I wanted a shower after such an energetic afternoon. 'It's been peaceful without Linden, hasn't it?', she said.

'Don't you like her?'

'We're very different,' said Dilly diplomatically.

'She's good fun,' I said, defending her, after all, she is Red's sister.

'She's just always rude to me,' said Dilly. 'And I can't trust her. I mean, why did she say that about Red to your Dad? Quite apart from her trying to get off with Charles last night. By the way, Flavia's terribly shocked – she takes herself and Red ever so seriously, when it's obvious he's nuts about you, but she can't cope with her little brother and sister fancying people. She complained all the way through our ride this morning!'

'Have you any idea when the O'Neills are coming back?'

'None whatsoever.'

'Have you ever met the great man?'

'I think we had dinner with them and some other people last year. Why?'

'What's he like?'

'No less normal than the other people here. I mean he is about the most famous film director in the world – as Linden never tires of telling me. I don't think he has much in common with Mum and Dad to be honest, but hardly any one does, unless they happen to live in the identical corner of Warwickshire as we do, and since we own most of it there aren't many who fit that description.'

'I like your Mum and Dad. I've never met anyone like them before. Your mum reminds me of Penelope Keith!'

'They're OK. They don't fight or anything like that. It's just that they're out of the ark – time-frozen somewhere in the 1930s – long before they were born even. That's what comes from generations of a family that has always lived in one corner of Warwickshire. Flavia's a great one for saying why change if you don't need to. And I suppose I am too, sometimes. But I do *not* want to be like Flavia!'

We'd come to the point where our ways parted. 'See you later,' said Dilly. 'Hope you find Red. I have to wait until the morning to see Charles. Holly told Jonty they'll be on the beach early because they're going on some outing tomorrow.'

'See you,' I said and went to our rooms. It was very cool and peaceful. I grabbed a banana from the fruit bowl and opened the balcony windows. I ate the banana and looked out over the tropical garden and the pool to the sea. People were making their way back to the hotel. Loads of them change for dinner – you should see them, they look as if they're going to meet the Queen! I'm just so annoyed I forgot to pack my tiara! You know, I shouldn't be at all surprised if the Hayters really have them. I must ask Dilly some time. I've never met anyone as posh as her before, but she's just nice and normal underneath. I'm not so sure about Flavia though. Fancy owning a large part of Warwickshire and coming here every year. And skiing at Easter. And sometimes New York for Christmas – or the flat in Chelsea. Unbelievable. I can't wait to tell Mum and Eloise about them all. And fancy rubbing shoulders with Oliver O'Neill! Mum will be gob-smacked. Talking of the O'Neills . . . I really want to see Red tonight – *alone*. For at least five minutes. I wonder if that will be possible?

I had a shower, washed my hair and changed into one of my little clubbing dresses – a shimmery strappy number in a soft rose colour that I know suits me, especially when I'm brown. I thought I'd look nice for dinner with Dad, to make up for our row last night. I know he's trying. And I'm still really touched by the fact that he's laid on this fabulous holiday just for me.

I dried my hair, made up and put on some jewellery that my ex gave me. He had surprisingly good taste and it all looks even better with a tan. I went down to wait in the bar for Dad, and had myself a little fruit cocktail (or FC as the Hayters would call it). The sun was setting on a perfect evening and the palm trees were waving in the gentle breeze. *Honest*! The bro-chures do not lie on this matter! I finished my drink but there was still no sign of Dad. I didn't see anyone I recognised. The Hayters must have gone somewhere else. Perhaps the O'Neills weren't back yet. I waited a bit longer. I wondered if he'd left a message for me in reception.

I went to the desk and the receptionist told me to

look in our pigeon hole. There was a fax message there! It said DUMONT on it and our room number. I read it, but it was *for* Dad, not from him, from someone called F. Marchant. It said, 'Will Saturday ever come? Grantley Adams 5.00 p.m.' I re-read it. God knows what it meant, work no doubt, but I didn't quite like the sound of it and I'm ashamed to say I crumpled it up and tossed it in the nearest bin. Dad's fault for not being here.

'Maddy!' I looked up, and there was Red. He must have just spotted me, because Linden and Oliver were walking on through reception. 'Did you eat dinner?' His eyes burned into mine as he spoke – it was lovely. I was so pleased to see him.

'No. I'm waiting for my dad to get back from golf. I thought he'd be back hours ago. And I'm starving!'

'Right. Maddy, quick. Come with me.' He checked his back pocket. 'Mobile. Dollars.' He took my arm and hustled me out to the front of the hotel where a taxi was still ticking over. 'Good. This is the one that just dropped us.' He pushed me in and told the driver – 'Carambola please!' and then sat back and dialled the hotel. 'Hello? Message for Richard Dumont from his daughter: Gone to Carambola with Redwood. Home by eleven.' He laughed at my surprised face. 'I'm not Oliver O'Neill's son for nothing you know. I like to make things happen.' He started dialling another number. 'Hi, Dad. It's me, Red. Change of plan. I'm eating out. See ya around eleven.'

He looked at me appraisingly. 'You look stunning! Now listen. I have it on good authority that the golfing party got a little held up and won't be back at the hotel until nine at the earliest. I saw Jonty, you see.'

I felt breathless. 'What's the Carambola when it's at home? Should I be screaming? You know what Linden told my father—'

'Though I'm embarrassed to say it, yes, I do know what Linden told your father. Jonty also informed me of this. The Carambola is an extremely trendy place to eat, but the reason I want to go there is because it's the best place to watch the flying rays. Our taxi driver was telling us they were good tonight on our way back to the hotel. So you can scream if you want to, but I shouldn't bother because we're nearly there.' The taxi had climbed to quite a height and drew up outside a restaurant on a cliff terrace. We got out. Red paid the driver and asked him to come back at 10.30. *So* efficient! *So* unlike my previous boyfriends!

'Dad will be furious.'

'Well, he's no right to be. He was late and didn't tell you. He knows where you are. Forget it. Enjoy!' And he put his arm around my shoulders and steered me in.

We found a table that overlooked the sea. Red quickly ordered us the set menu and some mineral water, so we could stand up and follow where people were pointing. And there they were! Silver-backed in the twilight, giant rays broke through surface and flapped across the water. At first you saw nothing and then you saw one and then another and another – it was magic, like looking for stars in the evening sky.

'They are just so outta this world!' said Red with a happy sigh. 'And we can still see them if we sit down. Great. I last got to see them when I was too young to appreciate it, you know? And another time I pestered Dad to bring me here and we were too early. Linden was quite little and we had to go back. I was real angry.' He smiled at me. 'I hope you didn't mind me kidnapping you, Maddy. You looked so pretty standing there, and kinda forlorn, that I wanted to whisk you away. Especially after last night.' He took my hand in both of his. 'Later, huh?'

And then, guess what. His mobile rang! 'Linden, hi. Yes. Sure I know what I'm doing. Yeah, I woulda taken you, but it wasn't like that. Now you know where I am and who I'm with so you don't need to ring again. In fact – Linden? Linden, I'm switching off. Messages only, OK? Bye!'

Our food arrived. It was all beautifully arranged on the plate and the cold drinks came in an ice bucket. I still have to pinch myself (just above the inside of my knee where it really hurts) to believe all this and remind myself that I'll be back to pot noodles when it's all over. We were both ravenous and spent a while stuffing our faces.

Then Red turned to me and said, 'You know, I cannot believe I just did that – kidnapped you.'

'Feel free,' I said. 'Any time.'

'I just *so* did not want to miss the rays, and I kinda wanted to see them with you – and there you were.'

Hey! He wanted to share things with me, just like I wanted to share them with him!

'I'm really sorry about my dad last night. He thinks he's protecting me.'

'After what Linden said to him, I cannot say I'm surprised! You know, I guess *she* thinks she's protecting me and Dad, in her way, by scaring people off. Not that it works with Dad – it is not unknown for him to take advantage of his position. That's why my mom moved us a few blocks down. She is so totally different from him.'

'What does she do? Is she an actress, like my mum?'

'Mom? No way! She's a shrink! No shortage of work for her in Hollywood – though she's a child psych now. Ironic, considering Linden.'

'What do you mean?'

'Linden's so like Dad. Mom's real steady and sensible, – ha! like me, I guess – and Dad's the opposite. A few years ago, when Lin was twelve or so, and cranky, she really hated Mom and moved in with Dad – a few blocks away. Mom didn't stop her, but it was a disaster. Dad had another girlfriend who did not want Lin around. So Lin came back, but for a while she'd only talk to Mom through me. Mom thought it wisest just to let her get through it. They're OK now, but Lin feels she has to keep tabs on me and Dad all day long. It's time she grew out of it – and got on with being a nice kid, you know?'

'I like her.'

'She's OK – but I think that says more about you than her. And I don't want to talk about Linden any more. I want to know more about this golden-eyed English girl with a face like an angel, who dances like a dream. Where have you been all my life, Maddy?'

'Living with my mum and little sister in a London suburb and going to the local comprehensive.'

'A what?'

'A big state school.'

'I can never work out your British education system. Don't you call private schools public schools or something?'

'This is not a private school – it's more like your high school. Twelve hundred kids.'

'So you're an English schoolgirl, huh? Do you get to wear a uniform?'

'Enough, Red! I'll start to think you're kinky! And no, we don't have a uniform – sorry to disillusion you!'

'And your dad? Has he remarried?'

'No, he hasn't married again. My mum left him for another bloke and they had my little sister.'

'What's your stepfather like then? Is he a nice "bloke"? (I love that word, "bloke"!)' Red laughed.

'Well, it's complicated you see. Mum left him, too, for another bloke that lives down the road. I don't like him much – the new one, Roddy.'

'Sheesh! Today's kids really suffer for their parents, don't they? I'm not complaining though. Mum's cool and so's Dad.'

'What's it like having such a famous dad?'

'People always ask that. Basically he's just my dad. For a while I was embarrassed about it but now I'm real proud of what he does. He's very dedicated and very focused. It gives me a real buzz to watch him in action. He loved those tango shots by the way.'

'You showed him?'

'Why not? They were fantastic! Jonty was such a shock, man! I took that guy for a total jerk when I first met him, but now – he is so cool. So British. Your genuine article.'

'They're seriously rich, the Hayters.'

'What the hell! So am I! We wouldn't be eating here if I wasn't. Does it bother you?'

'No, just makes me jealous. Since I am seriously poor.'

'And seriously, seriously beautiful.' He found my hand and stroked it. I still couldn't believe my luck – this amazing guy, who I fancy like hell, fancying me! I mean, it hardly *ever* happens that way, does it? And no Dad, and no Linden. 'What say we go outside and look at the view from there?' Red asked, fixing me with that piercing blue gaze. 'It's a while before our taxi arrives.'

I followed him outside. It was dark and quite steamy – clouds covered the moon and it felt as if it might rain. The tree frogs were very noisy. Red held my hand as we stood looking out over the black sea and then pulled me to him. 'Would you object if we carried on where we left off last night?' he said (ever the gentleman).

'I'd object far more if we didn't,' I said, and reached up to kiss him, feeling I'd explode if I didn't.

. . . And explode if I did. Red is *dynamite*. He's *really* really strong with broad shoulders and fabulous wind-surfer's pecs. I didn't stand a chance! I had to lean back against a tree for support! I could have gone on kissing him for ever, in fact I would have done. But Red was whispering into my ear, first something about how it was a good thing we were in a public place or he wouldn't trust himself not to answer to Linden's description and then, 'Don't look now, but I think we've been rumbled. Your dad has turned up.'

This was ridiculous. *Just* as things were getting interesting. Red gave me a big sexy squeeze and then straightened out his clothes. 'Go to the bathroom and sort out your lovely face and your mussed-up hair,' he said. 'I'll go find your father and reassure him that all is well. We don't want to antagonise him.'

'It's just so frust*ra*ting!'

'At least we're agreed on that. Go *on*, or the sex maniac will attack again and your father will have real grounds for anxiety!'

I went to the ladies and looked at myself in the mirror. I was very flushed. I splashed cold water on my face. That was better. I took a deep breath. Wow. I'd have to watch myself with Red – it wasn't *him* I was worried about. A romance is one thing, but this is like a – a – *jugg*ernaut. What do you *do* when you like someone so much and they like you back? All I want is for us to curl up together out here on the cliff and stay all night. Oh well. It's not to be. I'll go quietly, Dad. This time.

Seven

To be fair to Dad, he'd come out to the Carambola partly because he felt guilty about getting back late, and partly because when he picked up my message they told him that I'd picked up an earlier one and he wanted to know what it was. 'I'm sure whoever it was will fax again, Dad – I honestly can't remember what it said. Anyone important would double-check wouldn't they? Might it have been someone called Grantley Adams?' We'd said goodnight to Red (Dad even gave us a couple of minutes to ourselves while he paid the taxi driver) and Dad and I were in our rooms having drinks from the mini bar.

'That's the name of the airport, airhead!' he said. He was going to say something else, but he stopped himself. 'Did you see the rays at the Carambola? I saw them last year – terrific sight, aren't they. Quite romantic, as I remember!' He gave me a quick smile. He really *is* trying! 'I must say, I find it rather endearing in the boy that he wanted to see them.'

'Red's really keen on wildlife. He does underwater filming according to Linden.' I said. 'Imagine growing up with all that sort of equipment there for the asking. It does seem unfair sometimes.'

'Talking of The Great Man – I get to meet him on Thursday. A couple of them are going to join me and Brian for golf.'

'Wow, Dad. Do you think he might offer you some scriptwriting?'

'Different league, darling. I'm not distinguished enough for him to know me by name.'

'Gina Hayter knew your name, didn't she though?'

'Ah, that was for a different reason. Now, since I'm your father, I think I should probably tell you to go to bed. But do what you like – as long as you stay up here. I'm whacked, so I'm hitting the sack.'

'I'll stay up for a bit. I just feel like looking at the sea. I love our rooms here, Daddy – just you and me. And you can relax tomorrow! Red and Jonty are going windsurfing on the east coast, so you won't have to worry about me one little bit. I intend to catch up with Holly and co. on the beach.'

I woke up early and lay there thinking about my lovely Red. He is *so* gorgeous looking and *so* kind and *so* sexy and so – *everything*. I really think I'm in love. I sort of want to be with him all the time but then again I don't mind *not* being with him if I know I *am* going to be with him later. I don't have that scary feeling you sometimes get that if you're not with your boyfriend all the time he's going to find someone else, or go off you or something.

I got up and dressed for a morning on the beach. I remembered what Dilly said about the cricketers being down there early, and hurried over for breakfast. Dilly was racing through hers on her own. 'Want to get down there before Linden,' she said. 'I don't think she knows they're going off later. You coming?'

I wrapped up some fruit in a paper napkin, grabbed a croissant, and followed her out. I'm sure it's not how civilised guests behave, but tough. Our speed was rewarded. There were the boys, and Holly, and no Linden. 'You're so lucky, Holly,' said Dilly, 'being with this lot all the time.'

'You wouldn't think so if it was you,' said Holly. 'Anyway, I could say the same about you being with Jonty all the time!'

'Hmm,' said Dilly, and they both laughed. Dilly, tanned, with her hair tied back, a discreet amount of gold jewellery and a *really* expensive bikini, looks less and less horsy than my first impression of her. And I like her. She's funny and she's self-aware. 'Now help me, you two,' she said. 'There's to be no escape for Charles!'

'I happen to know,' said Holly, 'that Charles is very susceptible to flattery. He doles it out so much himself that it comes as a shock when the compliments are aimed at him. So how about – er – "I really like your shades / boardies / sixpack / haircut / eyes . . . tan?" '

'But I like *all* of them,' said Dilly plaintively.

'Ask to borrow his goggles, or something,' I suggested. We had to get the girl to him somehow. 'Charles!' I called. Dilly shrank. 'Charles, come over here! Dilly wants to ask you something!'

'Madd*y*!' Dilly hissed.

'Just think of something, anything,' said Holly, starting to giggle.

'What? What do you want?' Charles looked at us

suspiciously. And then, bless him! – 'That's a cool bikini, Dilly,' he said.

Dilly opened her mouth, but no words came out. Charles sat down beside her, and in a flurry of sand and sunscreen bottles Holly got up and grabbed my arm so we could run off and leave them together. We raced to two empty sunbeds under a beach umbrella and collapsed onto them. 'Well done, us!' said Holly. 'They just needed that little extra push, didn't they?'

'I hope they get it on before Linden arrives,' I said. 'She's going to be at a loose end with Red and Jonty on the east coast, so it's only a matter of time before she finds us.'

'Don't forget we're all going off in an hour – to Harrison's caves – so Charles won't be here. Neither will I. You'll have her all to yourself!'

'That's OK really. If we go back to the pool Dilly can keep the Flavour company and I can be with Linden.'

We looked over to Charles and Dilly. They were wandering down to the water together. 'Ooh, look!' squeaked Holly. 'They're going for a swim together! How sexy!' They disappeared into the waves and bobbed up again a few metres away, Charles in hot pursuit of Dilly. 'Lucky things,' said Holly. 'Why aren't Jonty and Red here – we ought to be frolicking in the sea with them, too!'

'At least we can indulge in girl-talk,' I said. 'That's almost as much fun as what they're doing.'

'Almost,' said Holly. 'Especially if you tell me in *great* detail all about last night.' So I told her about Red

kidnapping me and going to the restaurant and watching the rays.

'And then?' she asked. 'Did you finally get to kiss
him? I bet he's incredibly sexy! You can tell, just by
looking at him. I mean, he's all fit and hunky –
magazine stuff. Well? Did you?'

'*Yeah*,' I said.

'And?'

'He was a*maz*ing,' I said, and fell back in a pretend
swoon on the sunbed.

'Maddy!' she said, pretending to be cross. 'Don't stop
there! I mean, did you – *do* anything else? Or did you
just kiss?'

'None of your business!' I said, and swatted her. 'But
we were out on the cliff terrace with loads of other
people! It was a public place.'

'Oh,' she said, disappointed. 'I'd like to be in a very
private place with Jonty. And I was hoping you might
be able to give me the benefit of your experience . . .'

'You have to go at your own pace,' I said, realising I
sounded very *old*. 'And that's the problem, Holly –
with Red. I've got this feeling that Red's and my pace is
a bit too hot for comfort. I just *know* we both really
fancy each other – it's not as if he's rushing me or
anything. But I don't know whether we should try to
keep the lid on it, or not. Especially with Dad and
Linden on our case all the time.'

'Seems like circumstances are going to hold you
back, for the moment anyway. What, with Red not
here today, and Linden following you everywhere, not
to mention your Dad. My problem is getting to be with

Jonty at all – the Beale boys' schedule is quite hectic, and he has stuff he wants to do with Red. I keep wondering if we'll be able to see each other when we get home. We might live in different worlds, but at least it's the same country!'

Dilly and Charles were coming up the beach hand in hand. 'Aaah!' said Holly, and nudged me. The other cricketers were beginning to get up and go. 'Looks like his time is up!' she said, getting to her feet. 'I don't suppose I'll see you until the morning again – but I shall want to know *everything* this time! And you, Dilly!' She turned to Dilly who was rubbing herself down with a towel. Charles had gone to join the other boys. Dilly had a *big* smile on her face.

And not even the sight of Linden making her way towards us across the sand could wipe it off.

The three of us – me, Dilly and Linden – wandered back up to the pool. Dad was there, so were the remaining Hayters. Oliver O'Neill and his entourage were out in force, too. Dilly said, 'Catch you later,' with a mean-ingful look – she wasn't about to discuss Charles in front of Linden. I waved at Dad but dived into the pool with Linden. It's uncanny how like Red she looks. And that's the closest I'm going to get at the moment!

We climbed out and sat on the side with our legs dangling in the water. Linden, unaware that Dilly had finally snatched Charles (as if she honestly cared any-way), was all American good humour. We chatted the rest of the morning away – I was really interested to hear about her life because it was Red's life too.

We had lunch by the pool and afterwards Bianca's parents came down without her and joined us. They had left Bianca sleeping, with one of the hotel's nurses in charge. 'We can't expect you to be the only one that gives us a break!' said her dad. 'In fact she's still exhausted from yesterday. I can't tell you how thrilled she was. I don't think I've seen her so happy for ages – and that's thanks to you, Maddy.'

I offered to read to her tonight – people don't believe I really get a buzz out of it, but I do. After lunch Dad came windsurfing with Linden and me – he wasn't bad at all – and we spent the rest of the afternoon flopping about on the beach and dipping into the sea. It was all totally laid-back and relaxed – just how a holiday should be.

I went up for a shower and then went to read to Bianca before supper. 'Maddy!' she snuggled up against me. 'Will you tell me a story about Bianca and the banana boat tonight?'

'OK.' Her mum and dad joined in and helped me elaborate on the story. I felt pleased that I'd had the courage of my convictions and made it special for her. There wasn't any talk of dying or sadness tonight, though I suppose it hung over them all like a cloud the whole time. One the positive side, they were working hard to make happy memories for themselves. One day all this would be distilled into a small golden Bianca era, captured on film and video and in their heads. Concentrated.

I went out to find the others for supper feeling elated but raw – a strange emotional combination. And there was Red, waiting for me! Ooooh! He caught me up in a wonderful hug – all warm and rugged and lovely aftershave smelling. 'I want to walk along the shore in the sunset with you,' he said. 'I've been thinking about it all day while I was out on the water. And when we've had some time alone together I'm happy to join the others, but not until then, you know?'

'That's fine by me,' I said, 'But how *do* we avoid the others?'

'Easy! We head out the front and round the side.'

We did just that, stopping to kiss every few moments. It felt so right – when Red held me it was as if we were two halves of the same person. We took our shoes off and walked along the edge of the waves in the sunset. Most people had gone up for dinner so we had the beach almost to ourselves. I thought of storing up memories and decided to fix this one in amber. Red held me at arms' length and smiled. 'I'm just so – happy!' he said simply, and then pulled me to him again, and we stood ankle-deep in the shallows. 'I know we only just met, but I never felt like this before about anyone.'

'Me too,' I mumbled into his shoulder. We kissed some more and clung to one another – I really didn't want to meet up with the others right then. I wished Red and I had somewhere to go, but we didn't. My dad was expecting me, and no doubt Linden would be calling Red on the mobile any minute now.

Bang on cue, his phone rang. 'Tell Dad I'll be there in a coupla minutes,' he said to her, no more.

'C'est la vie,' I said with a sigh. It was no bad thing to

be leaving the sand – lots of little crabs were coming out and going about their business. Was *everything* conspiring against us?

'Tomorrow,' he said, 'I'm not going anywhere. And I know both our fathers are playing golf. How about we just lie out on towels all day? You oil my back and I'll oil yours? Cool off in the sea together?'

'Sounds perfect,' I said, and wondered why my voice wouldn't come out properly. He squeezed my hand and went off to where Linden was waving. I saw Dad coming in with the Hayters and went to join them.

And perfect is how the next day was. Red and I took the cushions off a couple of sunbeds and put them next to each other. We bought some cool aloe vera stuff off a guy on the beach and rubbed it into each others' backs – *very* sexy. Then when we got too hot we just went into the sea and cuddled underwater. That was *very* sexy too. I knew we were storing up trouble with Linden, but we ignored everyone for most of the day. The cricketers also had a free day, so Holly and Jonty were able to be together and so were Dilly and Charles. Something in the water, obviously! Flavia appeared once, to boss Jonty and Dilly about, but stalked off, furious, when she realised that they were ignoring her, and went to be with her mother.

Red told me all about himself, his childhood, his ambitions to make wildlife documentaries or set up a watersports school. I just love everything about him. I can't bear to think about the holiday ever ending – so I won't.

I told him more about me and Mum, Eloise, Gus and Roddy, even my old friends, Sophie, Hannah and Charlotte. He says he can't wait to come to England to meet them all – he's travelled a lot but never been to Britain. He has a lovely way of looking at me when I talk to him, and stroking my arm or my hand, my hair or my face, as if he never wants to let go. We didn't bother to go up for lunch – in fact we fell asleep in the shade. I woke up to see Red so close, his eyelashes on his cheeks. I didn't want to move but Jonty broke the spell when he and Holly came by kicking sand on us and offering to bring us back some drinks. Then Red's phone rang. I answered it. It was Linden being dangerously nice, she'd bagged us some seats in the beach bar. I told her Red had fallen asleep and that we might see her later, but I could tell she wasn't pleased. I couldn't blame her really, but it had to be *her* problem, not mine.

Jonty and Holly came back with the drinks and Red sat up and rubbed his eyes. 'I need to cool off and wake up,' he said. 'Maybe we could go for a bit of a windsurf later on?'

Jonty looked enthusiastic, but Holly quickly said, 'You mean with Maddy, don't you Red?'

'Definitely with Maddy,' said Red smiling. 'I want to do *everything* with Maddy. You know?'

'Blimey,' said Jonty. 'Thank you for sharing that with us, Red, but you didn't have to.'

Holly cuffed him. 'You know that isn't what he meant, Jonty,' she said. 'I might have thought twice about you if I'd known you had such a dirty mind,' and she dragged him off, leaving me and Red to wander hand in hand down to the water.

We went windsurfing in the afternoon together, Red helping me to do it better than before – he's a really good teacher. 'I'm going to take you scuba diving one of these days,' he said. 'There's so much to see. We won't go very deep or anything, but I guess I just want to show it to you.' So that's something to look forward to.

We went back to our place under the beach umbrellas, and there was *Linden* lying out on one of the sunbeds. All good things have to come to an end, I suppose. Linden was being fine – it's just that she was *there*. Soon after, Jonty and Dilly joined us too.

We all went up to the hotel for showers. Linden was trailing behind Red and me, practically treading on our heels. We were about to go our separate ways when she came out with a Linden-special and said to her brother, 'Now don't go thinking you can sneak off to Maddy's rooms with her, Red, just because her father's away. I know he'd disapprove, wouldn't he Maddy?'

'I never even considered it,' I said. I hadn't.

'Oh leave us alone, you're embarrassing us!' said Red. He looked uncomfortable.

'I'm off,' I said.

'So are we,' said Dilly. 'They won't be late back from golf, tonight. It's only just down the road a little way. See you all later!'

Dad came in soon after. I was drying my hair after my shower. 'That was terrific!' he said, throwing himself into a chair. 'Apart from the fact that I haven't seen much of my darling daughter!' He poured himself a drink.

'Well I had a lovely day, too!'

'Did you sweetheart? Good. By the way, you've got a fan!'

'I know. Red.'

'No, I don't mean Red. Now don't let this go to your head – but it's none other than Oliver O'Neill.'

'In other words, Red's father – he approves of his son's girlfriend does he?'

'I don't know that he's aware you're Red's girlfriend – but he's seen you dancing on video and he thinks you're – now, what was his word? *Sensational*! Yes, that's it. He asked me if I was the father of the *sensational* English girl! I shouldn't be surprised if he asks to see you before the holiday's over.'

'He's seen me already, Dad. What do you mean?'

'You know, *see* you. Casting. *West Side Story* and all that.'

'Oh Dad, don't be a silly old proud dad. I mean, *do*, but don't go giving me ideas! The school production is quite enough of a challenge for me, thanks very much. And I know all about Oliver O'Neill and his casting couch.'

'What *do* you mean?' He realised what I meant. 'Oh *honestly*, Maddy! I'm sure Oliver's not like that. He's far too professional.'

'Well, whatever. I'm glad it gave you two something to talk about.'

'Now, I was thinking it was time you left the hotel

and saw something of the island. How about you and I go off somewhere tomorrow?'

'This isn't a ploy to get me away from Red, is it Dad?'

'No, not at all. You can bring your friends if you like. I just want to spend some time with *you*, before – before the holiday ends.' Dear old Dad. I suppose we haven't spent much time together so far.

'As long as I can see Red in the evening! Let's just go together, Daddy. You see, Dilly and Jonty will want to be with Charles and Holly if they possibly can, and Linden gets really narky when I'm with Red. I suppose it could just be Linden, but perhaps if she has a whole day with her brother all to herself she'll lay off a bit.'

'Whatever you think is best as far as your friends are concerned, but I thought we could go to Harrison's Caves. In fact, I expect the others have all been before anyway. I went last year and they are quite an experience.'

Eight

Red was *so* disappointed (it was very gratifying) when I said I was spending the day with my dad, but he agreed that I ought to see Harrison's Caves, and cheered up at the prospect of being together in the evening. 'Except—' he started.

'What is it?'

'Well, it was Linden's idea in the first place – after Jonty's Latin dancing display – that we should all go along to this swanky dinner dance in the hotel tonight that the olds are going to – you, me, Linden, Jonty, and I suppose the other Hayters. Whaddya say?'

'My father won't know what's come over me, wanting to go to something like that, but yes, OK. I'm on. I like dinner and I like any sort of dancing. *Especially* with you.'

'My feelings exactly. Any opportunity to hold you close in a dimly lit place – and on this occasion it will be sanctioned, you know? So long as you do not go smooching with anyone else.'

'Oh yeah, Red. *Who*, precisely?'

Dad and I caught the bus after breakfast. It was the first time I'd been away from the hotel other than when Red kidnapped me and took me out to the Carambola. Quite apart from anything else it was good to see real Barbadians, going about their business – not just a whole load of horribly spoilt white people getting burnt and getting drunk. OK, the holidaymakers aren't all like that, but it must look like it sometimes. Dad said I mustn't forget that Barbados needs its tourist trade, but I still feel uncomfortable with it. Politics isn't my thing, but getting under other people's skin is what acting is all about – so I can't help thinking that way.

Inland the island is quite flat and green. You forget about the sea and the sand. And then it started raining! It chucked it down, and the bus splashed its way along the narrow roads. People on bicycles were soaked through, though no one seemed to mind or be surprised. So most of my view of this wet world was accompanied by the rhythmic beat of the windscreen wipers. It made me feel melancholy, and reflective. I kept thinking about how this brilliant holiday would end and become a bright memory that contained Red like a glowing star, and about how it would be the same only a million times worse for Bianca's mum and dad. And then I thought about Mum and Lo-lo and our comparatively grey and struggling lives – most people's lives in fact. And then I suddenly felt a rush of affection for Dad – after all, I only had *him* for this fortnight too. I clutched his arm and rubbed my head against his shoulder.

'Hey,' he said. 'What's all this?'

'Love you, Daddy. I suddenly felt all sad about us only having another week together – and how I won't see Red after we go home and—'

'Mid-holiday blues!' he said dismissively. 'You'll get over him. That's the thing about holiday romances.'

I pulled away from him. 'Thank you for your sympathy, Dad! I suppose you think I'll get over you, too?'

'No, darling. Let's not get confused here. I'm your father. Red's just a lad you've met on holiday.' Dad was being very unsentimental.

'Two men I love,' I said, and started looking out of the window at the rain again. I felt hurt.

Of course the sun came out after a while and I can't feel angry at Dad for long. He seemed preoccupied, as though he had problems of his own, so I decided not to make a big deal out of it. The bus turned to go down hill and we rolled under a big wrought iron arch that welcomed us to Harrison's Caves. 'This will be worth a hundred geography lessons,' said Dad, as we put on hard hats and climbed aboard the special train. I'm not altogether happy about confined spaces, but Dad said I would be far too interested to feel claustrophobic. He was right. It was *weird*. The train rumbled along and then we came out into what was like a vast underground palace, all on different levels, with waterfalls and cascades and lakes. It was cleverly lit up, but there were still dark shadows and all those pointy bits – sorry, stalagmites (mites grow UP) and stalactites (HOLD ON tight) – that looked like carvings in stone. We drove on and down and twisted round bends. It wasn't scary exactly, just eerie. I felt as though Dad and I were in another world – a fantasy world, like in *The Hobbit*, and that we might never leave it. He could be King and I'd be Princess and all these people would be our subjects, but we'd never get out and see our families or friends again – no Mum, but no vile Roddy either. No Red, but no annoying Linden. Weird thoughts in a weird place.

The rushing water was terribly noisy – it made your brain do funny things. The guide was giving us information about how the water carved all these shapes out of the limestone, and the amount of time it took for the pointy bits to build up. Everyone was oohing and aahing and flashing their cameras or rolling their camcorders. I felt stranger and stranger.

'*Amazing*, isn't it?' said Dad. 'Aren't you glad you came?'

'Yes, but it makes me feel *odd* being down here. Another planet altogether.'

'I know what you mean. As if the real world didn't exist. Sky and clouds are just something you made up.' It's obvious that Dad and I often think alike.

At last we emerged. We'd only covered a mile, but it seemed like a much longer journey. The heat and the bright light as we came out burst onto us like an explosion.

We went into the restaurant. 'I fancy a pizza please, Dad. Something to make me feel real again. I feel so weird today – you and me on this tiny island thousands of miles from home. I don't quite know what's brought it on. Suddenly everything seems so – fragile.'

'Sit down poppet – I'll go and get us some pizza. I'll be back in two shakes of a puppy's tail.' He was talking to me like a child and I found it reassuring. This oddness had to do with Red, I was fairly sure. I felt safe with *him* – I felt safer with him than my own dad. Why? I couldn't explain it. I felt tiny, so small, as if I was sitting in the palm of someone's hand.

Dad came back with the pizza. 'There! Good old pizza. That should feel like home. Perhaps you've been eating too much seafood or something else exotic. Are you feeling a bit better now?'

'Yeah, yeah. I'm fine really – I don't feel physically ill – just odd. Anyway, my strange mood has passed now. What do we do next?'

'Wander round here for a bit? Drive around in a bus and have tea somewhere?'

'Fine. You've heard about tonight, haven't you?'

'I gather you young ones might grace the dinner dance tonight with your presence. It's a good job I'm willing to pay for you. You do know it's *dead* posh – don't you? If I go I have to wear my DJ.'

'Cool. Does that mean Red and Jonty will have to, too?'

'Oh yes.'

'I'm sure I can borrow something from Dilly or the Flavour, or even Linden.'

'You'd make any dress look glamorous.'

'OK, Dad, I'll wear my little clubby number shall I?'

'Better stick to the dress code just in case they decide to impose an age limit too, though I think you'd be able to get away with most things. I can't see them turning you away.'

'So long as I have the long gloves? I forgot to pack them as well as the tiara – oh no! You'll have to take a photo of me, Dad, for Lo-lo.'

'Of course I will. I'll want one for myself, won't I?'

We seemed to bumble about on buses all afternoon, but it was fun. Some of the buses were really crowded, but Dad and I got a seat together again on the last leg of the journey back to the hotel. He leaned towards me and cleared his throat. 'Today wasn't an attempt to keep you away from Red, Maddy. You know that, don't you?'

'My decision entirely.'

'But—' he coughed again. 'You will watch yourself, won't you darling?'

'Da-ad. Say what you *mean*!'

'Well, I know I've left you alone quite a bit—'

'That's been good for both of us.'

'Well, yes. But you wouldn't – wouldn't *abuse* the fact that I'm not around, would you? I mean, you and Red wouldn't slip upstairs . . .'

'Dad! I hadn't even thought of doing that. Well, not until Linden suddenly came up with it last night.'

'Ah.'

'Dad – did *she* put the idea in your head?'

'Well, she did just say something – not quite within earshot, I must admit.'

'Dad. Listen. Will you just see things from my point of view – just for a moment. OK? Now – Red and I have just met. We like each other very much. We're getting to know each other. We need time alone sometimes. It's all very new. I don't *know* where it's going! I don't *know* if it's going to last! I don't know *anything* yet! But what I can't stand is other people jumping to conclusions about what we're getting up to. It's none of your business – or Linden's! No wonder we need time alone.'

'Maddy! You know and I know that what we're talking about here is sex.'

'Precisely. Which is why it's no one's business but our own. Dad – we have been lectured at school, I talk to Mum, I read the advice in magazines! I am not ignorant. Red is not my first boyfriend. But give me credit, will you? These are *my* decisions. Some adult having sleazy thoughts about my private life is pretty disgusting really. I don't do it to you!'

'While you are still a minor, and very much a minor, it *is* my business! What would I tell your mother?'

'Oh, get off my case, will you, Dad? Treat me as a human being in my own right, not as just another one of *your* problems. Mum always says that every person and every relationship is different – you can't make the same rules for everyone. It's like speed limits. If there's no one around and you're on the motorway you go at 90, I know you do.'

'That's quite different. No one's going to get pregnant at 90 miles per hour.' He was deadly serious of course, but it made me giggle, and then he saw the funny side of it and we both managed to laugh as the bus pulled up near the hotel.

Dad and I went in search of the others and found them on the beach. Jonty, Red and half the cricket team were stripping off their T-shirts suggestively and waggling their shorts in Full-Monty fashion, while singing 'I believe in miracles', to a hysterical audience, including Bianca and her parents. My dad turned to Holly's dad – 'Kuh! Kids today, eh?'

I felt as though I had been away from Red for a week. 'I missed you so much,' he said. 'I had all these horrible feelings about how it was going to be at the end of the holiday.'

'Me too,' I said. We were walking along the beach. 'Let's not spoil our time together, Red. We have to think of it a bit like Bianca's family – except that there's a possibility we *will* have a future.'

'Speaking of the little lady,' he said. 'She and I are as close as *that* now,' (he linked his little fingers) 'She was dancing for me on the beach and I videoed her. She played to the camera like a dream.'

'She must be feeling well today!'

'Her mom and dad said she was having a good day. And now – what about *my* dancing girl?' He put his arms around my waist and lifted me right off my feet.

'Glad to be back. It was interesting, and it was nice to be with my dad. But he got quite heavy – about us, actually – and that was a drag.'

'What do you mean, heavy about us?'

'Oh, never mind.' It was as if precisely what I'd been talking about with Dad was happening. Other people speculating about our relationship could tarnish it. 'I can't wait to see you in a tux, Red. Do you really own one?'

'Part of the famous film-director's family uniform. Linden has a glitzy dress or two as well.'

'I feel like Cinderella! I don't possess anything that glamorous. I'm going to have to ask Dilly or Flavia.'

'One of my father's friends will have something, I'm sure. There's one I like – Tricia – who must be about the same size as you. Probably why I like her! She has good taste. She'll be only too happy to do a favour for the Great Man's son.'

'Red!'

'There have to be some compensations! She'll be by the pool, I figure. Let's go find her.'

Tricia was sophisticated New York Chinese and slim as a whippet. I could see why Red likes her. She's cool and intelligent as well as being stunningly beautiful. And far from treating him like the Great Man's son she acts like he's a friend of hers. 'Sure!' she said. 'Maddy, you're so pretty you'd look terrific in a dishcloth, but you're welcome to try some things on. D'you want to go choose something now? I was getting bored down here anyway.'

'Go on, Maddy,' said Red. 'I can't wait to see you.' He was all excited, like a kid. (I had a moment of thinking – look at us Dad, Red is thrilled because I'm going to wear a gorgeous dress – allow us to be this innocent.)

My wardrobe in my hotel room is a vast empty space with a few little dresses and tops languishing on hangers at one end. Tricia's on the other hand, is *bursting* with dresses, blouses, skirts, suits, trouser suits, tennis gear, aerobics gear and *ballgowns*. It's like Eloise's Barbie wardrobe. Plenty of 'dining outfits' here. 'Wow!' was all I could say.

Tricia started pulling hangers off the rail and laying dresses out on the bed. 'Your colouring's kinda golden,' she said. 'Hmmm. Now, green looks good on honey blondes. And so does red. How about this one?' It was divine – simple, with thin, thin straps and fitted like a corset at the waist. 'I'm sure it will fit. Try it.'

I went into her bathroom and climbed into the dress, then made an entrance into the bedroom, walking towards her long mirror. Tears sprang into my eyes when I saw my reflection – I realised it was a

RED dress, a red dress for Red. And I've never felt so beautiful in all my life.

'My turn to say Wow,' said Tricia. 'In fact I have to sit down. Maddy, you look *gorgeous!* And Red, my favourite young guy in the world, will love it. Hey, you're *perfect* for each other.'

'Can I borrow it, then?'

'With pleasure, honey.'

Dad was straightening his bow tie when I went back to our rooms. 'Weyhey, Dad. You look cool!'

'Not so bad for an old guy, eh?'

'Not bad at all. But just wait until you see your little girl in this dress.'

'A princess, I'll be bound.'

'Will you wait for me, Dad, while I shower and change? I'd feel a bit shy going out all dressed up on my own.'

'Of course, I'd be delighted to escort you.'

I had a shower, shaved my legs and under my arms – you can't hide anything in a dress like that – washed my hair. I rubbed half a ton of body lotion into my skin, dried my hair, put on the dress and spent a while on my make-up. The lipstick was a problem – what colour lipstick do you wear with a red dress? I ended up just wearing loads of gloss. I sprayed on a bit of glitter and squirted scent on my neck and pulse points. 'Come on!' Dad was knocking on the door.

'OK Dad, hold your horses.' Shoes were my last problem, but actually my strappy sandals looked fine. I stepped back to look at myself in the full length mirror. Yup, I could go to the Oscars with Red dressed like this.

'Ta-dum!' I threw open the door.

Dad looked at me long and hard. He coughed once or twice before he passed judgement. 'Your mother always looked beautiful in red – not many women do. You look absolutely fabulous, darling!'

'No kidding?'

'Absolutely no kidding.'

Red looked so handsome in his tux and DJ I practically fainted. His eyes were glistening – because he said *I* looked so stunning! But *everybody* did! Even the horsy old Hayters were in their element. Gina and Flavia were dripping with jewels as well. In fact Flavia with her hair up looked incredibly grand – she's well on the way to owning half of Warwickshire already (it's probably dangling from her ears and nestling in her cleavage at this very moment)! Dilly had the good taste to stick to something plain and gold . . .

Oliver O'Neill wore evening dress as if he wore it *every* evening and looked very film-starrish. He and his entourage had a table to themselves but Linden and Red sat with us. Linden is very pretty whatever she wears, but her dress was fussy – I felt more elegant in the simple red gown.

It was a brilliant evening. Red's not a bad dancer and I took a few turns with Jonty (for sheer class) and my Dad. I even had a dance with the Great Man. 'I hadn't realised the little tango dancer was the young lady who's turned my son to mush,' he said. 'But I can see why!' And he smiled down at me with all his smile lines crinkling. Red looks very like him, but more honest somehow. Oliver held me rather tightly to dance – I was glad to escape from him.

'Dad never dances with *me*,' said Linden. 'You should be flattered.'

Red and I managed to nip outside on our own for a bit. 'I'm taking pictures of you in my brain,' he said (when we came up for breath). 'No film could capture how you smell,' he sniffed at my shoulder, 'or the golden-brown softness of your skin,' he stroked my neck.

'You old romantic, Red.'

'No, I mean it Maddy. I'm crazy about you. Sometimes it seems unbearable,' and his eyes really did fill with tears as he kissed me again. So did mine. I couldn't believe my luck. It all seemed too good to be true. We stayed out there for quite a while – at least until Linden discovered us.

'Come back in you two,' she said. 'Don't abandon me to Flavia and Cordelia.'

'You've got Jonty to talk to,' I said. 'Think how jealous Holly must feel tonight!' But we went back in. A steel band had replaced the more conventional dance band and everyone was boogyin' on down, so we threw ourselves into it, collapsing back at our tables to cool off and have a drink. Linden was really quite drunk and Flavia, her hair starting to come down and her lipstick smeared, was getting frightfully sloshed. Dad was very merry and so were the Hayters. Gina had a bright glint in her steely gaze as she drew deeply on her cigarette in its holder. The music went all slow and smoochy. Red and I were about to get up and dance when Linden said, 'Hey, Maddy. You weren't here today so you won't know. Guess who's coming tomorrow?'

'How can I?' I said. 'I don't know anyone.'

'Come on,' said Red. 'Let's dance – it'll be over soon.'

'Well at least we're spared Matty-Matt, aren't we Richard?' She looked at my *dad*. Since when has Linden been on 'Richard' terms with my dad?

'I – er – believe Fay Marchant is coming on her own,' said Dad.

'Maddy. Come and dance,' said Red urgently. 'Please.' So I was able to lose myself in Red and forget what Linden had said for several hours.

Nine

I woke quite late to hear Dad clattering around. It sounded as though he was tidying up and rearranging the furniture. I turned over and tried to get back into my dreamworld – a re-run of all the best bits of last night. But it was not to be. Dad knocked on my door. I grunted. He took that as a signal to come in.

'For heavens sake, Maddy! It's nearly eleven o'clock!'

'So?'

'High time you were up, my girl.'

'Da-ad.'

'Things to do.'

'Dad. I'm on holiday. We had a late night last night.'

He stood up and looked around my room. The bright morning sun came in through the gaps and illuminated the make-up and tissues and cottonwool balls on my dressing table, the clothes I'd stepped out of on the floor, and the trail of towels, hairbrush, hairdryer from when I'd been getting ready. Nothing unusual.

'This room is a disgrace!'

'Calm down, Dad. I'll tidy it up. I always do.'

'They will have stopped serving breakfast hours ago.' He was like one of those horrid little wind-up toys. Natter natter natter.

'Dad! Sit down for a minute. I'm awake now – not that I want to be. What is all this about? Are we expecting visitors?'

Dad sat down. I had a sudden cold sensation. Something was wrong. There were things I didn't know. Phone messages. Half-finished sentences. 'Dad – is there something you haven't told me?'

'Nothing that need bother you, darling.'

'Well, it's sure as hell bothering *you*, so what is it?'

'All right. I'll come clean. My friend Fay is arriving today. I'm meeting her at the airport this afternoon.'

'What's this got to do with me getting up and tidying my room?'

'I – want – the rooms to look nice when she comes,' he said carefully.

'She doesn't need to look in my room, does she?'

He didn't answer straight away. I sat up in bed. I felt

sick now. A realisation was dawning. 'Dad. I've twigged. That's it, isn't it? "Your friend Fay" is your *girl*friend! She's not coming to visit us – she's coming to *stay!*' I prayed that he would contradict me.

But he didn't. He wriggled and squirmed, but he didn't say it wasn't true. 'Well, yes. She'll stay, but it needn't affect you, darling.'

The crassness of those words. 'DAD! NEEDN'T AFFECT ME!'

He tried. 'Well, nothing will change. You'll still spend time with me and with your friends. It'll be just the same, except that Fay – will – er – sleep here.'

I shook my head in disbelief. I felt like a maddened bull or something, shaking my head from side to side. I was sitting crosslegged on my bed now, and I found myself rocking backwards and forwards as I shook my head, thinking, 'NO! NO! NO! My special holiday with my dad. His little princess. These lovely rooms all to ourselves. It isn't all for me at all. How *could* he think nothing would change. How *could* he!' I started to cry.

'Maddy – sweetheart!'

'How *could* you, Dad! You made me believe this was all for *me*, and it wasn't. It was for her.'

'I wanted you to meet her,' he said lamely. 'She wants to meet you.' He put his arm round me, and tried to stop my shaking sobs. 'Please don't be so upset, Maddy. I wanted to come back here, see Fay again, and I wanted to have a holiday with you. Is that so terrible?'

I was too upset to answer. If he couldn't see that I felt betrayed by his not *telling* me, there wasn't much point in saying anything. I put my feet back under the bedclothes and curled up, snuffling. Dad tiptoed out and left me. My untidy room had ceased to be an issue.

Half an hour later Dad knocked on my door again and came in with a tray of fruit and rolls. 'I don't know what to say, darling. Just, please, give Fay a chance. Give your old dad a chance. OK?' He set down the tray and left again.

I picked up the phone by the bed. Red's mobile number was written on my hand. 'Red, I need you. Something awful's happened. Where are you? Down by the pool? I'll see you there in a few minutes.' I didn't bother to shower. I just took off all the make-up I should have removed last night, put on my bikini and shorts and ran out. I was red-eyed and I felt as if I'd been crying all night, but seeing Red would have to help a bit.

Red saw me approaching and came over in his swimming shorts to meet me. He gave me a slippery hug – 'Factor 10 hug, that is!' he said, to make me laugh. 'I'd just put it on.' I managed a feeble giggle. 'So what's happened? Nothing to do with Bianca I hope?'

'No. No. It's not that awful really. Well it is to *me*, but I suppose it could be worse.'

'Well?'

'It's this Fay woman. She turns out to be Dad's girlfriend. She's coming today and she's going to be sharing our rooms.'

'It *could* have been worse, then,' said Red, trying to lighten up. 'She could have brought Matty-Matt with her.' But he could see that I wasn't laughing – even the implications of a Matty-Matt were ghastly. They didn't bear thinking about. I tried not to remember the conversation the others had had about him in the beach bar. We sat by the pool. I had to cheer up because Dilly and Jonty were pleased to see me, and Linden was there too.

'Good dancing last night,' said Jonty.

'You looked fabulous in that red dress,' said Dilly.

It already seemed a lifetime ago.

'Flave has a terrible hangover this morning,' said Jonty, nodding in the direction of Flavia, who sat fully clothed in the shade wearing a turban and sunglasses and looking pained. On the table beside her were two bottles of water and several sorts of hangover cures.

'Linden is a bit the worse for wear, too,' said Red. 'She's more cranky than usual.'

'We're off to the beach now,' said Dilly. 'We're meeting Charles and Holly there. See you later!'

'Come in the water,' Red said to me. 'It will cool us off, and we can talk.' We slipped into the pool together and swam to the other side where it was empty.

'Perhaps I'm being selfish about Dad,' I said. 'But I'm hurt that he didn't tell me. No, it's more than that – I'm hurt, full stop.'

'I hate to see you unhappy,' said Red. 'It's not how I think of you.'

'No one can be sunshine and light all the time.'

'Of course not. I've seen you serious, just not unhappy. I've got a lot to learn about you.'

'And not long to do it!' I splashed him and dived underwater so he'd chase me, and we came up together, laughing.

'That's better,' he said. 'Forget about your dad while you're with me. Please?'

'I intend to,' I said, and swam off again, with him in hot pursuit.

I did intend to, but Linden came and sat with us when we climbed out of the pool and she seemed determined to keep the subject uppermost in my mind.

'So you get to meet the mother of Matty-Matt today? Wow!'

'I'm reserving judgement,' I told her.

'Well, as we all know, she just *adores* teenage girls!'

I wanted Linden to leave off. But she wouldn't. 'I kinda remembered that she and your father were an item,' she said.

Red said impatiently – 'How could you have done, Lin? Maddy's father wasn't staying here last year when we were. It was the Hayters.'

'Oh, something Dad said,' said Linden vaguely.

'Great,' I said crossly. 'So everyone except me knew that Fay was my dad's girlfriend. No doubt everyone except me knew that she was coming today.'

'Oh yes, I knew,' said Linden. I could have hit her. I jumped into the pool instead. She came after me. I climbed out and she followed me out. 'I don't know why you're upset,' she said. 'My dad has women staying with him all the time. And not always the same woman.'

'Well my dad DOESN'T! OK?'

'Leave it out, Lin,' said Red. 'Can't you see that Maddy's upset?'

'I would be too if Fay was going to be *my* stepmother, I suppose,' said Linden.

I was ready to kill Linden. I went ice cold. 'Shut up Linden. You don't know what you're talking about. Go away and leave us alone.'

She looked at me and she looked at Red. 'Beat it,' said Red. I would have said something far worse, but I didn't need to, because, eyes blazing, she turned on her heel and left.

I started to cry again. 'I'm sorry about Linden,' Red said. 'I told you she was cranky today.' He hugged me. 'Hey, look who's coming! This will cheer you up. Howdy Bianca!'

Bianca was being carried down to the pool. She waved like crazy when she saw us. 'Maddy!' she called. 'Did you know that Red is *my* boyfriend now? I'm going to be a film star and marry him!'

'Puts it all into perspective, doesn't it?' Red whispered. 'Hi, girlfriend!' he said to Bianca. 'Coming for a swim then?'

Red was right. Bianca always puts everything into perspective. So although the word 'stepmother' was grinding away in my brain, we managed to spend the next hour very happily with Bianca before going to the beach bar for lunch.

Dad was there. He sat up at the bar amongst all the semi-clad holidaymakers dressed in a pressed shirt and trousers and cleanly shaven. He looked nervous. 'What do you two want to drink?' he asked as we came up to the bar. 'I'll get these while you sort out some food for yourselves. Here are some dollars, Mads.'

'Thanks, Dad. You're looking very smart! Not as smart as last night, of course.'

'I'm going to the airport in a taxi. Don't want to be too scruffy.' He waited for the drinks while we ordered food and came back to sit down. 'OK, I'm off now.' He kissed me goodbye as if he was leaving for ever. And I suppose, in a way, he was. Our holiday *a deux* was over. 'We'll all meet up for supper. Fay will need to settle in first, so – 7.30? In the dining room bar?'

'Red, did *you* know Fay was coming?'

'Yesterday Dad took Linden and me out to lunch with that woman who was talking to your dad at the barbecue – Meryl. She's a screenwriter he works with. She said something like, "Did you know Fay was coming tomorrow?" I went off to the mens' room at that point, but she must have said something about her and Richard – your dad – while I was away, because Linden picked up on it on the way home.'

'So you *had* heard!'

'You know Linden! She was the one going on about "Fay and Richard", oooh poor old Maddy. I just assumed she was winding me up. She does it all the time. So yeah, I knew Fay was coming. I knew she had some connection with your dad. I did not know she was staying with you. There! Am I forgiven?'

'I just hate the thought of being the last to know.'

We had reached the beach. I was trying not to think about dad, but it was impossible. The thoughts just wouldn't go away. Holly and Jonty were there with Dilly and Charles.

'Wait here a minute!' said Red. 'I'm gonna fix us up a boat. I'll be back.'

'Ace idea! I'm coming too,' said Jonty, and ran after him.

'Hi, Maddy,' said Holly, giving me a girly hug. 'I feel as if I haven't seen you for ages. How was Harrison's Caves – and the posh dinner dance? I've heard all about *that*! Linden said you completely silenced everyone at one point because you looked so stunning and you're such an amazing dancer. She said her dad was all over you, wants to sign you up for his film.'

'*Holly!* You know not to believe a word Linden says! She was blatantly winding you up because you weren't there with Jonty and she was!'

'Dilly said you looked fantastic too.'

'OK, so I borrowed a fabulous dress. It was *red*, Holly! Don't you think that's romantic? Red for Red? I was with him most of the evening – God he looks *gorgeous* in a tux. Can you imagine?'

'I can. And how did Jonty look?'

'As to the manner born. You'll have to get him to invite you to Flavia's ball!'

'Do you think he would?'

'Can you imagine that he *wouldn't*?'

'Oooh.' Holly went all starry-eyed.

'Linden's winding me up too, at the moment,' I said.

'Really? What about?'

Suddenly Holly was the best person in the world to be talking to. 'Have you got five minutes? An hour? A lifetime?'

'I haven't got anything else to do!'

'Well – you know how I was really excited about this holiday and being just with Dad and all that? Well, now it seems that some woman is going to be with us for the second week. His girlfriend. I didn't know he had one.'

'What? He never mentioned it?'

'Not once!'

'Bummer!'

'It is pretty poor, isn't it? And Linden somehow got to know because the woman, she's called Fay, has been here before – I think Dad might even have met her here – and the others all think she's awful. She's got this monster of a son called Matt.'

'Oh yes. I've heard stories about Matty-Matt. He was here with Jonty and Red last year wasn't he?' Then she opened her mouth and put her hands to her cheeks. 'Oh NO! She's THE MOTHER!'

'Thanks for that, Holly.'

'Eughh!'

'Precisely. And Linden goes on about how she wouldn't like to have Matty-Matt's mother for a *step-mother*!' I could feel my throat closing up and tears coming again.

Holly saw. 'Oh Maddy,' she said, and put an arm round me. 'It's not funny is it?'

I snivelled. 'No. It's a nightmare.'

'Oh poor you.'

'Red's asked me to try and forget about it while I'm with him. But I can't forget it Holly, how can I? It's like Dad saying it needn't affect me! What are men made of?'

'They just don't like being troubled by women's emotions. It's nothing new.'

'Red's being really kind otherwise. And I don't want to spoil our time together.'

'You two are really perfect for each other, did you know?'

'You're the second person to say that. I think so too. Do you think I've met him too early in my life?'

'Oh no! You can marry him! I'm going to marry Jonty!'

'And be very rich?'

'And be *very* rich!'

Jonty came running up at that moment and announced that they had a boat for the six of us – Red was getting it ready. So we spent a really great afternoon on the water. Red knows how to sail like I know how to dance – he was lovely to watch. And, guess what – I really didn't think about Fay. Perhaps Dad was half right, at least. I *can* still spend time with these friends. They are almost as important to me as him now. And, sorry Dad, but Red is more important to me now than *anyone*.

I changed for dinner. *I changed for dinner!* I felt as nervous as Dad about meeting this Fay. I waited for him in the bar. I had my *West Side Story* to pass the time. I sat over my fruit cocktail, reading 'Te adoro,

Anton.' Of course it's all about love and families and death. Right up my street these days. A man slipped onto the bar stool next to mine – 'Dad!' But it wasn't Dad, it was Oliver O'Neill.

'Drink?'

'I've got one thanks!' (Duh!)

He smiles his crinkly, blue-eyed, sun-tanned smile. He still has good teeth. He's like Red but not like Red – it's very odd. 'What are you reading, then?'

Aagh. *'West Side Story.'*

'A *script!'*

'Yes, it's because—'

'I only cast professionals, you know.'

'It's nothing to do–'

'Does Red know about this?'

And this is when Dad and Fay choose to roll up, followed by Red and Linden. Red is smiling sympathetically at me. Linden is doing a silly walk behind Fay. Oliver knocks back his drink, nods at Dad and Fay and herds his children away from the bar. Dad and Fay sit down with me.

'I think that's the lad who had to beat poor old Matty-Matt at everything last year,' said Fay, looking after the O'Neills. 'Doesn't he have some ridiculous name?' And she laughed with a snorting giggle.

Fay is too streaky blonde and too tanned. She has a face like a hamster and she wears too much make-up. I hate her on sight.

Ten

I said as little as possible during supper. I was aware of
the O'Neills glancing in our direction from time to
time. Dad and Fay were lingering over coffee when I
excused myself and ran up to my room. Fay's scent lay
on the air. Her jacket was thrown over the back of the
sofa. I felt invaded. I ran to the phone in my room
and phoned Red. 'Meet me out the front in five
minutes,' I said, grabbed the dollars left over from
lunch-time, left a message for Dad and went down
there to wait for Red, praying that he'd turn up
without Linden.

He did. 'What's up?'

'Get me away from here. From her. Can we just go to
a bar somewhere?'

'Sure. We can walk or take a taxi.'

'I've got some money.'

'OK. We'll take a taxi!' We drove towards Holetown
and got out at a bar Red had been to with Oliver. 'They
won't serve either of us with alcohol, you know.'

'I don't care. Coke is fine. I just need to get right
away from that stupid woman.'

We paid the taxi driver and went into the bar. It was
pleasantly uncrowded, with a couple of guys playing
music in the corner. It was nice to be indoors for a
change, *without* a sea view and without all the visible

signs of luxury that I was beginning to take for granted. 'Do I detect signs of jealousy?' said Red, smiling at me.

'Of Fay getting attention from my dad, yes. But unless *you're* planning on paying her lots of attention, no!'

'Your sense of humour has returned, though. Welcome back!' He gave me a hug and a kiss right there at the bar, to cackles and wolf-whistles from some of the old guys there, before ordering a couple of cokes.

'You want me put some rum in that?' asked the barman. More cackles.

'No sir, we're fine, thanks,' and we went and sat down. 'Nice guy.' He leaned back to admire me. 'Hey, you're looking pretty cool this evening!'

'I dressed up for dinner. Thought I ought to make the effort. Everything you all said about Fay was right, wasn't it? She's vile. I don't know what Dad sees in her.'

'They lose their good taste when they get older. My dad had plenty when he married my mom, but he never seemed to find it again!'

'Same with my parents.'

'If your mom looked anything like you – your dad would have been real proud!'

'I can't tell. Most of the photos of her at my age are black and white, and she had long hair with a long fringe, so you can't really see her face. Though Dad keeps saying things like, "Your mother looked good in red".' We were sitting very close to each other on a plastic covered bench. Red just kept looking at me as I spoke. Then he made me put my drink down so he could turn to face me and hold both my shoulders to kiss me. More cheers and cackles from the old guys.

'Thass one beautiful woman you got dere, maan!' 'You treat her right, maan.'

'I don't care if they're watching,' said Red. Then, 'Maybe I do. But what they're saying is true, you know? You're beautiful and I want to treat you right. Let's go outside, Maddy.' So to cries of delight and whistles we made our way out through the door. It was dark outside and there was an empty bench on the pavement where people walked by. We made ourselves at home on it.

'No Dad,' I said, 'And no Linden. But still nowhere to go.'

'Let's start walking,' said Red, 'and catch a bus back to the hotel. It's not that late yet.' So we set off walking in the dark, stopping all the time to hold one another and kiss. It was kind of exhilarating but desperate at the same time.

We reached a bus stop as a bus drew up, and it seemed silly not to get on it. 'Tomorrow,' said Red, 'I'm going to take you scuba diving. Did you know it's meant to be the sexiest sport there is?'

'No wonder Linden and I weren't suited!' I said. 'But yeah, Red, that would be brilliant. Anything to take me away from Dad and Fay!'

'Let's go in the morning then – give you an excuse to get away early.'

We were pulling up at the hotel. 'I wish we could be together until then,' I said. 'I don't want to go back to our rooms with *her* there.'

'You have to, Maddy,' said Red. 'Think of all the ructions if you didn't – not that any of my lot would notice if you came back with me.'

'Linden would,' I said.

'True. Anyway—' he kissed me goodnight in the foyer, 'See you at breakfast. OK? Breakfast – no later.'

'Yessir!'

I crept back to my room. I could hear Fay's awful snorting laugh from Dad's room. I shut my door hard so that they knew I was back and set my watch alarm to wake me in the morning. I dreamed of Red. I dreamed of us finding somewhere to be alone together. It was heaven, but when I woke I wasn't sure whether we'd had to die first to get there.

Dad and Fay weren't up when I went down for breakfast. I left another note after the one I'd written last night. 'GONE SCUBA DIVING. SEE U LATER, M xxx.'

Red was waiting for me. 'Let's get down there straight away. I've abandoned poor old Lin again – I just said I'd see her down at the beach – so we need to get going. I've got the underwater camera.' He patted the camera slung over his shoulder. He'd booked the boat, everything. He instructed me as carefully as the official instructor had – almost grimly.

'Now – we have to rely on each other down there. We can't call an ambulance if something goes wrong. We can't talk, so let's just run through those hand signals again.' And again – we went through them about five times. But I felt really safe with Red. It was comforting to know he was qualified. The boat took us out, and over the side we went, diving together. It was fabulous, the only two humans in a world of colourful fish, even a couple of small sharks. Scary! But Red had assured me they would leave us alone if we kept moving – and didn't cut ourselves. We swam side by side all over the coral reef – Adam and Eve in the octopus's garden! It was all so beautiful. When we came up I felt as though we'd shared the most incredible experience.

'Your life was in my hands!' said Red easing himself out of his oxygen pack.

'And yours was in mine! It was wonderful, Red. Can we do it again?'

'Sure! We have to get our thrills where we can!'

'Red!'

'Well, I spent a lot of last night wishing you were with me, and realising that it was impossible.' He held my hands. 'Around three a.m. I found myself thinking that perhaps the only way to be together was to – sounds dramatic, I know – but, kill ourselves! Around 3.01 I got a grip – but sometimes I feel that desperate, you know?'

I knew.

Linden was waiting on the beach. She looked at us accusingly. 'Why didn't you say you were going scuba diving? I've been stuck here on my own. That's when I could escape from that terrible woman and your father, Maddy.' Here we go. 'They were real worried about you. She was going on at your father about how she wouldn't let Matty-Matt run that wild. And Dad wants us to meet him for lunch, Red. He wants to talk to you. About Maddy I think. I expect la Fay has been moaning at him, too.'

'Surely not,' said Red. 'I'll go sort this out, Maddy. You come with me, Lin.' He pointed down the beach. 'I can see Holly over there! See you in the beach bar at 2.30 if we don't meet up before!' He said that looking over his shoulder. Linden was dragging him towards the pool and Oliver O'Neill.

Holly was alone. She sat on a towel, hugging her knees. 'You OK, Holly?'

'The Hayters have gone on a two-day cruise, did you know that?'

'No wonder Linden is bored. She says she doesn't like them, but she likes needling Dilly and she and Jonty get on OK. Well, I'm here now – and I'm very pleased you're here too.'

'How's it going?'

'If you mean with Dad's girlfriend – badly. Though I've managed to avoid her since supper last night.'

'How d'you manage that?'

'Red and I went out to a bar near Holetown last night and we went scuba diving this morning.'

'Bet that went down well!'

'Linden's already taken great delight in telling me how badly it went down. But I don't care. They're such hypocrites, adults, aren't they? They were far too interested in each other last night to know *when* I came in.'

'Aren't they just! Mum's starting to have a go at me

about Jonty, now. Ever since I've been interested in boys she's said why don't I make friends with some of the *nice* boys at Dad's school. But now *Jonty's* too posh for her. "Oh I think you'll find you don't have much in common ultimately, dear." We can't win, can we?'

I love being with Holly.

'So how *is* the romance with Jonty?'

Holly rolled over on to her back. 'Oh he's so *cute*, Maddy. I'm not sure that he's ever been out with a girl before. And my experience isn't vast, so neither of us feels pressured by the other. We just have a *lovely* time. It's amazing what you can get away with under water, isn't it?'

'Holly! I'm shocked!'

'I don't believe *you're* shocked. I mean, you can see the *smoke* coming off you two. That's how Jonty put it. He said he could see you and Red "smouldering" whenever the other one was anywhere near. He told me to "look out for scorch marks"!'

I sighed. 'That's how it feels. Sometimes when we're together I imagine we're about to spontaneously combust! Tricky though. All the adults keep saying how *young* we are. As far as I can see, if you're in love you're in love. It feels the same whatever age you are. Look at Romeo and Juliet. Weren't they supposed to be thirteen and fourteen or something? We're fifteen – well, almost – and seventeen. Positively geriatric.'

'Not compared to your dad and Fay.'

'Don't remind me.'

Holly and I missed lunch, but then I had to go and meet Red, and she felt she ought to check in with her lot. I hoped I'd managed to miss Dad and Fay. I had indeed, because Red had a message from Dad saying they'd gone off to play golf (so Fay is the golfing inspiration). Oliver had gone too. Red looked serious.

'What's up Red?'

'Maddy?' He swallowed. 'Just tell me. Going out with me has nothing to do with who my father is, does it?'

'What?' I'd never seen him like this before.

'I didn't know you'd asked him for an audition.'

'*What?*'

'He said you'd talked about it in the restaurant bar last night. You had a script and everything.'

'*What?*'

'And then Linden said—'

'*Hang on.* Hang on! *Linden said* . . . Since when have you believed what Linden says?'

'She said you'd told her you wanted a part in his film.' He looked at me anxiously.

'Red – I don't believe this. Do you really think I'd do a thing like that! That everything we've done together has been a pretence, just so that I could get in with your father?'

'It wouldn't be the first time it's happened.'

'RED!' I was horrified. Did he *really* think that?

'I'm sorry, Maddy.' He looked miserable. 'I didn't want to believe her.'

I grabbed his wrists. 'Listen to me.' I shook them up and down. 'I brought *West Side Story* to learn as my holiday reading because they are auditioning for the *school play* when term begins. Ask Dad, Holly, Dilly – anyone. No, don't ask them, *believe me*. I'm a good dancer and performer but I'm lousy at learning lines. I wouldn't *dream* of auditioning for an Oliver O'Neill film. Well – I might *dream* of it, but no more than that!'

Red looked mortified but relieved. 'Oh, thank God for that! I was so scared it might be true. That's Linden for you – at her worst! Twisting things. I just wish she wouldn't do it!'

'Red, how about spending this afternoon on the beach – just dipping in and out of the sea from time to time?'

'Fine.' He hadn't quite got over it yet. 'Maddy – there's more. You see, Dad thought he'd been a bit harsh with you yesterday, and he told me he thought you *might* have the right qualities after what he's seen of you on video . . .'

If I hadn't been so keen to get into the water, Oliver's words might have gone to my head. As it was, well, I didn't think about them again that afternoon.

I had to go back to my room. I needed a shower – and I had to get out of my bikini some time. I didn't want to go there. I hoped Dad and Fay were still playing golf but I couldn't be sure I wouldn't open the door and hear her ghastly laugh. They weren't there. I had the place to myself – I could see that they'd come back from golf and gone out again. Still her scent pervaded the whole suite. Her bits and pieces were everywhere – her camera, her book, her shoes, a pair of earrings. My room was the only place still my own, thank goodness. I sat down on the bed for a few moments, glad to be alone – even to be away from Red for a little while. I was appalled that he had entertained the idea *even for a second* that I might have wanted to be with him because of his dad. Some terrible insecurity lurking there. But then we're all full of insecurities, especially those of us whose parents have split up. One of the things about Holly and even Dilly is a sort of rock-solid stability that I envy. I mean, Mum has always been there for me, and it's obvious Red's mum has been for him, but somewhere, deep down, kids like us are always on the alert for something to go wrong. We can't help it. It's how we've survived.

Mum. I had a sudden urge to ring her. Did she know about Fay? Would she care or would she wish Dad well? I looked at my watch before picking up the phone. It would be five hours later there – midnight. Mum wouldn't mind. I dialled the code for the United Kingdom and then our number. The phone rang and rang and rang. Mum wasn't there. She hadn't even switched on the answer machine.

Dad and Fay were sitting at a table for three with an empty space. No Hayters. The O'Neills were part of a huge noisy group on the terrace. Linden saw me and waved, but dinner with our families seemed to be the way it was. I could see Red's back. I could tell even from this distance that he was charming Tricia. So. Dad and Fay, here I come. 'Sit down, love,' said Dad unnecessarily. 'We're just about to order.'

'Yes, sit down dear,' said Fay, even more unnecessarily. I bit back the retorts that were ready to come out.

'I'll just have the soup, Dad. I'm not very hungry.' I looked around the room and realised that I hadn't seen Bianca all day. It was too late now. Bianca. Eloise. Mum. 'I tried ringing Mum at home, but she wasn't there, Dad.'

Fay pursed her lips – she obviously didn't like me mentioning Mum in front of her. 'Oh, she wouldn't be,' said Dad.

'How do you know?'

'She rang last night.'

'Why didn't you tell me?'

'You were out.' Touché. 'And anyway, she wanted to tell you something herself. She said she'd ring you again.'

'I had a great time scuba diving with Red, Dad.' I thought I'd better change the subject.

'Ah yes. Now I think we should talk about that, Maddy. Fay says you should only *ever* go out with a proper instructor.'

Fay had to stick her oar in. 'I did say to Richard that I certainly would never let my fourteen-year-old out of my sight. Especially not at night. And certainly *never, ever* in the water.' She sniffed and took a sip of her drink.

I looked daggers at Dad. 'Dad and I have our own way of dealing with things,' I said stiffly. 'And, for your information, Red *is* a qualified diving instructor – has been for over a year.'

We ate our meal in virtual silence after that. So when Dad suggested that we all went to the bar together and then up for an early night – together – I could only conclude that they wanted to keep an eye on me. I was seething with anger, but too upset to argue.

Eleven

Mum. Mum. I had to talk to Mum. I wanted to tell her all about Red and I wanted to tell her about Bianca and I wanted to tell her about Dad's *vile* girlfriend. I wanted to hear her voice. It was seven a.m. Barbados time. Broad daylight, birdsong and surf noise outside. All quiet in our suite, thank goodness. It was twelve noon in England. I dialled our number. It rang – in the hall at home – four times and then the answer machine. Even a recording of Mum's voice made me feel a little calmer. I left a message. 'Mum, please ring me back. I have to talk to you. Don't worry, no one's ill or anything. Love you Mum. Love to Lo-lo.'

Then I settled down to wait. I padded around in my nightdress, helped myself to fruit and mineral water and turned on the TV, partly to drown out the noise of Dad and Fay waking up. The noise of the TV brought Dad out to the living room. Tee-hee. 'Bit early, isn't it? Are you going down for breakfast?'

'Sorry Dad. I'm waiting for Mum to ring me back. I've left a message on her answer machine. So I'm not going anywhere.'

He considered the implications of this. 'Har-rummphhh.' He tottered back to bed. I knew he wouldn't want me to have my phone conversation with Mum while Fay was around. I heard the shower going and getting up noises and then a rather cross-looking Fay appeared. She'd found time to shovel on the make-up, but her eyes were all small and piggy from sleep still, and her cheeks were puffier than ever. Part of me was looking forward to describing her to Mum. Mum would sympathise.

'Morning Fay!' I said brightly. 'You and Dad off for an early breakfast then?'

'Yes, we are as a matter of fact. I want to make the most of my time here. Life in the city is so stressful, especially as a single mother – I want to be fresh as a daisy when I get back to Matty-Matt.'

'Yes,' I said, 'Mum finds it stressful too.' That shut her up.

Dad appeared, his hair sticking up from rushing around. 'So what are your plans today, Maddy?'

'Nothing, until I hear from Mum. I want to know what she has to tell me. So I'm staying right here. You needn't worry about me. I've got plenty to eat and drink.'

They went to breakfast and came back but still no call from Mum. They were off for a quick round of golf followed by a few hours out on a boat which would include lunch. 'I was hoping you'd come on the boat trip with us,' said Dad unconvincingly.

'You'll enjoy yourselves much more without me,' I said.

'So are you just going to leave her here?' said Fay to Dad, as if I wasn't in the room. 'She might get up to anything, *anything* – and you wouldn't know! I wouldn't *dream* of leaving Matty-Matt on his own all day in a foreign country.'

'Dad trusts me,' I said through gritted teeth, 'Don't you Dad? I'll be fine. Have a nice time. See you when I see you.'

'Really Richard!' Fay just couldn't shut up. 'That's *far* too vague. I think Madeleine should be down at the pool when we return from our boat trip. Don't you, Richard?'

'I'm waiting for Mum to ring back,' I said. 'I'll see you later.'

Dad tried to pat my arm in a reassuring way, but I shook him off. Right now the two of them were welcome to each other. That dread word *stepmother* was beginning to haunt me again.

I enjoyed having the place to myself. I prowled around, even Dad's room I'm afraid. I looked at Fay's things. They were all nasty. Her clothes, her shoes, her make-up – they were precisely the sort of things Mum and I avoided. Horrible fussy bows. Two-tone loafers. Bright blue eyeshadow. Eugghh. Hate. Hate. Hate. I watched some more TV and ate some more fruit and some chocolate from the minibar.

The phone rang. Mum! It wasn't Mum, it was Red. 'Maddy! I'm phoning from the pool. Your dad said you weren't coming out! You can't spend all morning in your rooms! I want to be with you! Come down for a swim at least. Please! Oh, yeah. Linden says to come down, too.'

'Red – I really want to, but I have to speak to my mum and I left a message for her to ring me back. I'm sure she'll ring soon, and then I'll be right down. Promise.' I did want to be with Red, especially after our misunderstanding last night.

'Come to the beach bar at lunch, whatever. Oh – Bianca's here. She wants to talk to you.'

'Maddy! Maddy! Red has been towing me round the pool and I think I'm in love with him. Will you read to me tonight? I'm going to bed early because I've got to see the doctor tomorrow.'

''Course I will, sweetheart.'

'Here's Red again, Maddy. Byee!'

'See what happens as soon as your back is turned!'

'I'll be at the beach bar at lunch time then.'

As soon as I'd put the phone down on Red I missed his physical presence. It was as if I'd been holding something in my arms and then found I was only clutching the air. I wandered round the suite, willing Mum to ring. It would be afternoon at home by now. I picked up my *West Side Story* script and sat out on the balcony to learn it. I couldn't quite see the pool from there, but I imagined that I could hear Red laughing and Bianca squealing. I went through it and high-lighted all Maria's lines.

It was lunch time, getting on for *six* o'clock at home. What was Mum up to? I rang again and left another message on the machine, giving myself an hour to have lunch with Red: 'Ring me after seven, your time, Mum. I'll be waiting by the phone.' I had a quick shower, put on shorts and a bikini top and went out into the bright midday sunshine.

'Aaagh!' Red pounced on me. He'd been hiding in the shadows again.

'Just wanted you for two minutes *all* to myself, you know? Before we hit the full Hayter/O'Neill contingent waiting for us at the beach bar. The Hayters have just got back. I think they're all a bit curious about Fay.'

In the bar they were all waiting for me. 'You have to tell us everything!' said Linden.

'Any news of Matty-Matt?' said Jonty.

'Oh leave the poor girl alone,' said Dilly. 'It must be bad enough without us all giving her the third degree. AND –' she moved closer to us and further away from the group that contained her parents, Flavia and a young man ' – I have to divulge the important news that *Flavia's* found herself a *chap*!' I peered over at him. He was very small with a lugubrious expression. 'He's exactly like a man, only smaller,' said Dilly.

'He's a *jockey*,' said Jonty, and then practically fell off his bar stool laughing. Red caught his eye, guffawed, and joined in and soon Dilly, Linden and I were all doubled up in hysterics as well.

'He's apparently a very famous jockey,' said Linden. 'Dad recognised him.'

'I can't wait to see when they stand up,' said Red.

'He was at the dinner dance,' said Dilly – 'but everyone was far too busy watching you two to notice them!'

'It was her necklace,' said Jonty, eyes streaming, 'the long one that—'

'We know, we know,' said Dilly.

'Well, it was at eye-level for him!'

We giggled all through lunch like naughty school-children.

I looked at my watch. 'Two o'clock, Red. I have to go.'

'Oh, don't go!' said Red. 'Can't you just ring your mum on my mobile?' I was torn. It did seem a shame to waste even a second of my time with Red. But then Jonty and Linden were on either side of him.

'He said he'd go with *me*!' said Linden.

'Red, old fellow,' said Jonty parodying himself. 'Did you or did you not undertake heretofore to come windsurfing with me this afternoon?'

Dilly joined in. 'Let Linden go with Red, Jonty. The Beale boys had a morning match today, so they might have made it to the beach by now.'

'What about me?' said Red. 'Do I get a say in this? I was just trying to persuade Maddy to stay out here in the sun with me instead of waiting in a dark hotel room for her mother to ring.'

'Dark hotel room, eh?' said Jonty. 'I can't under-stand you not wanting to wait *there* with her, mate!'

Red looked at me in mock despair.

'Go windsurfing with Linden,' I said. 'Then every-body's happy. Call me when you get back. Mum's bound to have rung by then. Cheerio! I'm off to learn some more lines.' I called after Jonty, 'Say hi to Holly for me! She'll be ever so pleased to see you!'

Three o'clock. Eight p.m. at home and still no Mum. Four o'clock. The phone rang. It was Red, back from windsurfing. 'This is *so* not the way to spend our precious few days together Maddy. What are you doing up there?'

'Learning my lines for *West Side Story*. Mum hasn't rung me yet.'

'When does your dad get home?'

'Don't know exactly.'

'I'm coming up, Maddy. I'll test you on your lines or something. I'm walking as I speak. Hey! Look out from your balcony!'

He was just down below! 'Romeo, Romeo!' I started – and then, 'Hang on a second! Let's get the relevant version!' And then I sang the first two lines from *Tonight*.

'Wow!' Red scampered off, singing the same words a semitone up, and before I knew it there was a knock on the door.

I let him in. 'Red – I'll be in big trouble if my dad and Fay get back and find you here.'

'It strikes me you'll be in trouble with Fay what-ever you do, so just relax, would you?' He sat down on one of the armchairs and helped himself to a passion fruit. 'Mmm! Passssssshion fruit!' He slapped himself on the wrist and went into an English falsetto. 'Naughty naughty boy. Passsssssiion' (he hissed) 'is only for wizened *old* people in this suite,

Richard. Matty-Matt does not know the meaning of the word "passion" and neither should you. I would *never* let Matty-Matt know that I indulged in such a thing. He might realise I was a hypocrite or something.'

I threw several cushions at him. 'Throw me your script instead,' he said. Then before I could do anything he leapt to his feet and chased me round the room, scattering more cushions and newspapers, two mangos and a spectacles case. He lunged at me and caught me up in some heavy-duty kissing. Impossible to resist. We toppled onto the sofa.

A phone rang. 'If that's Linden—'

But it was my phone. I went over to answer it. Red lay on the sofa with his feet dangling over the arm, hands behind his head.

'Mum! At last!' It was slightly weird hearing her voice in the middle of fooling around with Red.

'I'm sorry darling – I've spent nearly the whole day at the hospital.'

'*Hospital*! Mum! Is Eloise all right?'

'Yes, yes. Everything's fine! Can't you guess what, darling? It was the antenatal clinic – I'm going to have another baby!'

'Whoa, Mum! Slow down! Say that again!'

'Well, I had to tell Eloise because of going to the hospital and everything. She's so excited. I thought you'd like to hear the news straight from the horse's mouth, so to speak, before Lo-lo told you!'

I didn't get it. Was this Vile Roddy's baby? Was I going to have to suffer more Vile Roddy as well as Vile

Fay? 'It's you and *Roddy*, Mum, who are having this baby?'

'Of course, darling. He's very excited because it's his first.'

I found myself shaking my head from side to side again. Red looked up, anxiously. He'd got the gist of the news from my end of the conversation.

'Well, hey, Mum.' I couldn't do any better than that. Not the way I felt inside.

'What about your news, darling? Tell me quickly before I ring off – I'm paying for the call.'

'There isn't much, Mum. It's not really important – not like your news. I can tell you in person on Saturday. This is costing a bomb. Love you, Mum. Love to Lo-lo.' I put the phone down and found I was crying.

Red came over to comfort me. He made me sit on his lap and cradled me like a child, stroking my hair and handing me tissues that he pulled from the fancy box on the table. Some went on the floor.

Suddenly Dad and Fay were standing in the doorway. It didn't look good. Two very scantily clad teenagers on the floor, surrounded by scattered cushions and tissues and newspapers.

'Well *really*, Madeleine!' said Fay. 'What did I tell you, Richard?'

'Maddy – I'm very disappointed in both of you. I think you'd better go, Red. I'll be speaking to your father about this.'

Red didn't lose his temper. He just said quietly, 'I'd appreciate it if you spoke to your daughter first, sir,' and left.

'I'll leave you to it, Richard,' said Fay and went into the bedroom, no doubt to plaster after-sun on her horrible boiled-lobster sunburn. Her nose would peel tomorrow.

'Maddy?' Dad actually looked sympathetic. It didn't take a genius to see I'd been crying once we were face to face.

'It's *not* how it looks,' I said, sniffing. 'Just take my word for it. Please?' I looked at him pleadingly.

'Why the tears, sweetheart?' He held my shoulders and looked enquiringly into my face.

I leant my head against his still-Daddyish chest. 'Mum. Her news. She's only having another baby. With Roddy. It's happening all over again, Dad, and I don't think I can bear it. It was so awful with Lo-lo in the beginning. And Gus was bad enough but Roddy's loathsome. What if he moves in?' Fresh sobs shook my body.

'There, there,' said Dad. 'Sweetheart, I'm so, so sorry. You really don't deserve it. How we've both let you down! *My* poor baby!' and he was pretty shaky too.

'Red came because he knew I was in a state.' That was near enough the truth. No point in confusing the issue.

'I can see that now. We jumped to conclusions too quickly, I guess. Let me go and put Fay straight. We don't want her thinking badly of you, do we?'

As if I cared. I found myself another tissue and picked up the ones that were strewn about the room. Red must have pulled out at least three for every one he gave to me. How dare they send him away like that. He was being so lovely. And he was so dignified.

I went into my room and called him up. 'Red?'

'Maddy! You OK?'

'I'm OK but I'm angry. You were so cool, Red. Anyway, Dad knows the truth and he's telling Fay.'

'Shouldn't you be reading to Bianca?'

'Oh my God! Yes! – Red, meet me after supper. Meet me by the children's pool. There won't be anyone there then. See you about 8.30?'

I splashed cold water on my face and put on a top and some long trousers. I knocked on Dad's door. 'Got to read to Bianca, Dad! See you at supper?'

Dad popped his head out. 'Yes, dear, fine. Fay's had a bit too much sun on the boat, so I don't think she'll be joining us.' Best news I'd had all day.

Bianca was already in bed. 'Can I have some *hospital* stories tonight Maddy?'

Hospital stories are healthier in Bianca's case than happy stories. 'Sure? Have you got Zo-Zo?'

'Mummy and Daddy hate going to the hospital, but I quite like it. Everyone's always so nice to me. But I'm not sure that they will be so nice to me this time!'

'Bianca! Don't say that! Why on earth not?'

She beckoned me close and then whispered in my ear, 'Because I think I'm getting a bit better!'

'But that's great!'

'Mummy and Daddy don't believe me – but just wait

and see when we get back tomorrow. Night night Maddy. Sleep tight!' And she snuggled down under her covers.

Dad didn't say much over supper. I sensed that things weren't going very well with Fay, and knowing how antagonistic I was towards her he didn't want to discuss it with me. I didn't want to dwell on Mum particularly either, so we ate in companionable near-silence which made me feel as close to him as I had all holiday. I met Red by the pool and we climbed up above the road and sat looking at the stars for a couple of hours. A quiet end to an explosive day.

Twelve

This is bizarre. Dad and Fay, Red and Linden, Jonty and me are all sitting on a bus going to Bridgetown for shopping and a trip in a submarine.

Fay woke up feeling just a tiny bit guilty it seems, after blowing us out, and in great pain from overdoing it in the sun. Ha, ha, serves her right. Needless to say, her original tan was fake. So she decided to make today her shopping day and suggested to Dad that they take me and some friends on the submarine – Matty had loved it last year. They fixed it all up over an early breakfast and Dad woke me with a cup of tea and the news that I was to meet my friends in Reception in half an hour.

I wasn't altogether sure that I wanted to be organised like this, but there wasn't much to be done about it. I called up Red on his mobile. 'Isn't this weird?'

'Your dad said he was real sorry about yesterday, you know? And that they wanted to make amends. I've never done the submarine thing – could be cool. Linden's happy to be with us all – so! And I'm happy as long as I can sit next to you! See ya!'

The Hayters were all going to watch Flavia's jockey in action, but Jonty was more than happy to come with us instead. The Beale College lot were doing the same trip, so there was a slight possibility that he might see Holly in Bridgetown, too. All in all, my objections seemed pretty feeble, so I did my best to suppress them.

It started off fine. I enjoyed sitting close to Red as the bus joggled along. Dad and Fay were sitting in front of us, not saying much. Jonty and Linden were being extremely noisy behind us. Jonty is one of the few people Linden doesn't feel jealous of. They were playing Spot the Banana (you shout Banana! whenever you see one), which had them both in fits – there were plenty to be seen – growing, being sold, being eaten – but it got pretty raucous, as you can imagine.

It was funny being in a town with shops and car parks again. The sunshine seemed much harsher reflecting off metal and glass, so it was a relief to dive into air-conditioned shops. Jonty and Red reached their shopping-boredom threshold in about two minutes flat, so we split up – me and Linden, Dad and Fay, Jonty and Red. The boys went down to the beach to go out on jetskis. The rest of us went in search of presents and souvenirs. Linden and I looked round some of the department stores, but there was nothing suitable there, so we wandered down to the market stalls. It was hot and crowded but I soon found a lovely sarong for Mum and a perfect little bikini for Eloise. I bought some bracelets for my friends. When Linden was busy looking through some CDs I bought a ring for Red too. Soppy, I know.

We wound up at the harbour café that was our meeting place some time before the others. It wasn't very nice – brash and noisy. Linden and I sat down outside with our Cokes. The sun beat down on us and my head started to ache.

'I told Red it was a bad idea to go up to your room when your dad wasn't there,' said Linden, starting a wind-up out of the blue.

'He wasn't in *my* room, Linden.'

'Oh no? I heard that Fay hit the roof!'

'Linden – I don't want to talk about it. This whole trip is by way of apology! Let's change the subject.'

But Linden was just getting into her stride. 'So are you going to audition for my dad's film?'

'No way, Linden. I haven't got what it takes.'

'He thinks you have. He told Red to tell you to ring him if you're interested, but I bet Red won't pass that message on.'

Red hadn't passed that message on. 'Red doesn't think it's a good idea.'

'Well, he wouldn't, would he? He wants you for himself!' she said with a sly smile.

'Linden – what are you getting at?'

'Nothing!' she sang – and slurped noisily on her Coke, rattling the ice cubes. 'Do you want another one?'

'Yes please.' Anything to get her off my back. Anything to make this headache go away. Does Oliver O'Neill *really* think I've got what it takes? Why hasn't Red told me? I don't really want a part. Do I? How would I call Oliver? I suppose he's got a mobile too.

Linden came back. It was as if she'd read my mind – witch. 'If you do decide to call Dad, his number's easy to remember if you know Red's – we three are all one digit apart. I could call him now for you.'

'NO! Linden, let me make my own decisions.'

'Sor-ry.' She sat back, clicking her fingers and tapping her feet to an imaginary song. She looked around. 'Hey! Here come the boys. They do not look happy.'

'Phew! We've been ripped off,' said Jonty, kicking out a chair and flopping down on to it.

'They saw us coming,' said Red, leaning on my back and putting his arms round my neck. 'Shame, because the jetskis were real *fun!*'

Jonty tossed a heap of small change on the table. 'Buy us a drink, someone. That's all I have left of my spending money. You buy me one, Red, it was your rotten idea.'

'OK, OK, man!' said Red and went up to the bar.

'It was your idea, too, Jonty,' said Linden, leaping to Red's defence.

'It's being ripped off that annoys me,' said Jonty. 'They had us down as *tourists*.'

'We are,' I said. I didn't like his tone.

'Not like some of these people—' Jonty took off his shades and mopped his brow.

Red put down their drinks. 'Well – prepare to like tourists on the submarine. We won't be able to escape them down there!'

'Hey, everyone!' I said. We were all very tetchy. 'Lighten up!'

Then Dad and Fay arrived. Fay was red in the face. She wore her sunhat at a rakish angle which made her look slightly mad. Dad had sweat pouring down his face and neck.

'Well, we've got Matty-Matt's present sorted out, so *that's* all right.' He was playing to the gallery, I knew, and it was a bit embarrassing.

'What did you buy him, Fay?' I tried to sound interested. The others were smirking.

She was only too keen to show us. She pulled a horrendous pair of palm-tree patterned boxer shorts out of a bag. 'These!' she said proudly. 'And this!' A T-shirt with "I heart Barbados" on it. 'And this!' An inflatable banana.

'Banana!' shouted Jonty and Linden together, drawing attention to our little group.

'Well,' said Dad, 'It took us two whole hours to buy those.' Did I detect a note of sarcasm in his voice? 'And I need a drink.' He looked at Fay. 'Pina colada?'

Fay was determined to be difficult. 'Don't you think we should be ordering lunch, Richard?'

'This is a bar. They don't do lunch.'

Ooh dear. This was shaping up to be a tiff. I didn't think my headache could stand it.

'Dad,' I said. 'Why don't we meet you at the submarine boat place? You two have your drinks and we'll sort ourselves out with burgers or something.'

'But shouldn't we all—' Fay's day out wasn't going the way she wanted.

'Good idea, Mads,' said Dad. 'Here's some money!' And he handed me a fistful of Barbados dollars. 'We're booked on the three o'clock submarine. See you there.'

'*Richard*!' we heard Fay saying as we left, 'Wasn't that rather a lot of money for burgers?'

'Rather you than me, Maddy,' said Linden.

'Shut up, Lin,' said Red.

And so it went on. We were all too hot. It felt thundery. I wanted to be just with Red but Linden was always there, needling.

The boat out to the submarine was a relief. It was shaded by a tarpaulin and the cool breeze on our faces was a treat. We passed a boat like ours coming back from the submarine, and before we knew it Jonty was standing up and waving his baseball hat. 'Holly! Holl-ee!' he cried. He sat down. ''Spose that's as close as I'll get!' he said, disgruntled, as the Beale College lot sped in the opposite direction. I'm not used to seeing Jonty like this – he's usually so even-tempered. 'They've only got two more whole days,' he said.

'Well we've only got *three*,' said Linden.

'Three? Is that all?' I couldn't believe it. Only three more days with Red. We were all cast into deepest gloom. Red held my hand very tightly.

The boat pulled up by the submarine and we were handed down the steps. It was like getting on a plane except that you went down instead of up. It was very narrow down there. I tried not to think about claustrophobia. All I wanted to do was cuddle up to Red and watch those fish go by, but he was entranced – glued to the porthole. 'Wow! This is excellent, man! I've never seen so many of those rainbow fish before. Look at that, would you!'

There were a couple of wrecks down there – great playgrounds for the fish – but they made me feel sad. I couldn't help thinking of *Titanic*. Dad and Fay were still tense – they obviously hadn't resolved their shopping squabble. My headache was getting worse and I tried not to think about being claustrophobic. Red was going on and on about blasted fish. I put my head in my hands and shut my eyes. Is this how a baby feels in the womb?

'Maddy! Maddy! Just take a look at that, man! Jeez, do I wish I had the camcorder!' Red was getting hyper.

'What's that one called, Red?' Linden was crowding me out.

'Something wrong, Mads?' Jonty saw I wasn't enjoying myself.

'I'll be fine,' I said, without opening my eyes. 'I'll just be glad when we start going up again.'

'Bad luck!' said Jonty. 'You're missing a treat!' He

pushed up against the porthole too. 'Wow! There's millions of them all around us! What are those ones, Red?'

I felt wretched. It seemed an age before the captain announced that we were going up again. Probably keeping my eyes shut made me more claustrophobic than if I'd had them open – at least I might have been distracted by the fish.

It was wonderful when we finally got out in the fresh air again, though the bright light did nothing for my headache.

On the way home in the bus Red still couldn't stop talking about the reef. 'Please Red,' I said. 'I've got a cracking headache and you're not making it any better.'

'Sorry,' he said shortly. 'I didn't know I was boring you.'

'That's not what I meant.'

'That's how it sounded.' He looked out of the window.

'Red – don't be like that.'

'Like what?'

'All grumpy.'

'Well, I feel like an idiot. I thought you were really interested too.'

'I am, Red. I just can't help thinking about my other problems and my head hurts.'

'For goodness sake, Mads. Let's find you a headache pill!'

'If only it was that simple!' I knew I was being peevish.

Red sighed. 'I'm going to find you an aspirin.' He stood up and pushed past me to Fay, of all people. I saw her delve into her bag and hand him some tablets and a small bottle of mineral water. He sat down by me again. 'Here!' he said. 'I saw her popping a couple in that bar in the harbour. I just know that you're not a natural grouch.'

'I don't know which came first – the headache or the worrying.'

'Maddy – *please* quit worrying about your parents – just for three more days? Then you can worry all you want!' It was meant to be a joke.

'Huh! Thanks.' I know I was spoiling for a fight. 'My whole world has been turned upside down, Red – twice – and you expect me to switch my feelings on and off for your convenience?'

Red didn't get a chance to defend himself because the bus pulled up outside the hotel and we got separated as we filed off. Fay's shopping bags were unwieldy and bashed up against people. It seemed as if none of us was speaking to the other. Actually, that's not true. Linden was bothering Red about something. My head was still busting and I was full of pent-up fury.

Red finally caught up with me. 'Please, Maddy, I *so* do not want us to—'

'Red! Red! Maddy! Maddy! I'm back from seeing the doctor!' Bianca's little face was alight, but her mum and dad looked as tired and drained as I felt. 'Maddy, will you read to me? Please? I've got to go straight to bed and I want some stories? Please?'

'Of course, sweetheart.'

'You don't have to, Maddy,' said her mum.

'No, I'd love to. I'll come straight away.'

'Maddy, please!' Red had a hold of my arm. 'Can't we just talk a minute?'

'Let me go, Red. I said I'd read to Bianca. She needs me.' And I went.

'Bianca thinks she's getting better,' said her mum quietly to me. 'Of course, she's not – but we're going along with it, obviously. I'd love to believe that positive thinking worked miracles!' She gave a sad laugh.

'Right, young lady! What have you chosen for me to read today?' Bianca was in such a good mood it was impossible to believe that there was much wrong with her. Except that she was physically exhausted. By the time I'd read her three stories she was flat out.

I went back to our rooms. Dad and Fay were offering each other drinks and nuts and being polite to each other. Fay had a scowl on her face. 'Who is that child with the strange haircut who is always so over-excited? Her parents don't seem to know the meaning of calm restraint. She's certainly got *you* wrapped round her little finger, Madeleine!'

My jaw dropped. How *could* this woman be so horrible about Bianca? 'Tell her, Dad,' I said. There was no way Fay could redeem herself now. 'I'm going to lie down, my head's killing me.'

As soon as I drew the curtains and lay down, the phone rang. It was Red. 'Maddy! Good, you're back.

Please can we go somewhere and talk? This is awful! I can't *believe* what's happening.'

'Red – seriously I have a terrible headache.'

'Then how come you were able to read to Bianca?'

'Red! You're not jealous of *Bianca* are you?'

'Only when she stops us making our peace with each other.'

'I can do without this, Red. I've got a headache now. Bianca needed me to read to her. Please.'

'And I *need* you to talk to me!'

I managed not to put the phone down but I was speechless.

'Maddy – I need to talk about this business of Dad's film, too.'

'You mean the message you didn't pass on. Well, you needn't worry, because Linden did. Red – I'll see you later. GOODBYE.' And I did put the phone down. First Dad. Then Mum. Fay, of course. And now Red. Everyone out to get me. I hate them all. And in that dire frame of mind, I fell asleep.

Late in the evening the phone rang again. I reached for it sleepily. 'Maddy, it's Linden. You've really upset Red, you know. You don't know what my brother gets like when he's really upset. He's gone off for a walk somewhere. I just hope he comes back, because if he doesn't, it'll be your fault.'

'Linden – I went to bed because I was feeling lousy. Red knows that. And I'm still feeling lousy, so get off the phone and let me get back to sleep.'

'He really doesn't want you to talk to Dad about a

part in the film, either. I think he's worried you'll make a fool of yourself. He was really mad at me for telling you, anyway. OK. I'll let you get back to sleep. Bye now.'

Needless to say, after that little tirade it was some time before I got back to sleep. Oh yes, and I hate Linden too.

Thirteen

When I woke up in the morning I had my period. That explained a lot. It was late and Dad and Fay had left a note saying they were off playing golf for the morning. I had a lovely bath, found some magazines, made a hot drink, took some fruit and put myself back to bed. Sometimes a girl has to pamper herself.

But then everything started coming back to me. 1. I've had a row with Red! How did that happen? 2. Mum is going to have a baby with the awful man from down the road. It's gross. How can I go back home to that? 3. Dad is forcing me to share *my* holiday with hamster-woman. Let's hope she's a bit past it for having babies.

I want to go home – but what *to*? I'm not sure that I want to stay here with Fay. Why oh why do adults do this to us? Why are they so selfish? I feel as if there's nowhere to turn. My own life is giving me claustro-phobia!

I sat up in bed and hugged my knees. I was frowning with concentration. At the end of all this, there was only *me*. Whatever my parents did, even if they died – especially if they died – I was on my own. *I* was all that really mattered to me. The older I got, the more I had to make my *own* life. These thoughts seemed very profound. I pondered them for a while. They were leading somewhere, and what they were leading to was Oliver O'Neill and a part in his film. Me! A film star! I could handle that! Hmmm.

Then I remembered Linden's bizarre phone call. Something about Red not telling me in case I made a fool of myself? How dare he! Why would Oliver have offered to see me if he didn't think I had something? I *would* give him a call, dammit.

The number was one digit different from Red's. I took a gamble on it being one higher.

'Hi, this is Madeleine Dumont—'

'Hello? *Maddy*?' Hell! It was Linden! I put the phone down and dialled the number lower than Red's straight away before I lost my nerve. I'm only calling the most famous film director in the world.

'Yes!' It was definitely Oliver O'Neill's voice barking in my ear.

'Er, hello. This is Madeleine Dumont. I had a message to call you.'

'Who?'

'Madeleine Dumont. Your son – your daughter told me you said I should phone you.'

'Yes?'

'About *West Side Story*. I'm a – a dancer.'

'And?'

Did he even know who I was? 'And you said you might see me about a part in your film. Your daughter said.'

'And you're a dancer, you say?'

'We have met,' I said cautiously. 'I'm staying at the hotel.'

'Uh-huh.' I got the impression he was doing something else as he spoke, making coffee or reading the paper.

'So when could we meet?' No point in being timid.

'Six o'clock. Reception.' He suddenly stopped being vague and went all businesslike. 'We'll pop out somewhere for a drink.'

I had a shower and dressed. I couldn't help feeling that I was doing something wrong. I wasn't convinced that Oliver O'Neill knew who I was over the phone. I'd said I was a dancer – but it didn't seem to ring any bells with him. Shouldn't he have said something like – 'Oh, Red's girlfriend!' or 'the sensational English girl' or something? And then I remembered Linden on the subject of her father and young women. But I didn't have to believe Linden, did I? Anyway. It was done now. Six o'clock.

It was nearly lunchtime and I wasn't quite sure what to do with myself. I'd somehow expected Red to ring me, but he hadn't. What was everyone up to? The cricketers and Holly? The Hayters? I felt isolated.

I forced myself to go out and down to the beach bar. I went via the restaurant, the pool and the beach. I saw no one I knew. Flavia was at the beach bar with her jockey. He still looked lugubrious but she was drinking a ridiculously huge pink drink and laughing her braying laugh. 'They're all off on the pirate ship!' she said. 'I always thought it was simply an excuse to get sloshed, but Ma and Pa insisted on taking everybody. Trying to cheer up my little sister and brother I think. Honestly, anyone would think they were in *mourning*, and their friends on the school trip haven't even gone yet!'

'Did the O'Neills go, too?'

'Yah. I think the O'Neill *kids* went.' (How long ago was it that she had been madly in love with Red?)

'Well, that's great. Obviously no one thought to tell me.'

'Someone said you weren't well. Your mother, was it?'

Flavia really was the pits. 'Do you mean my father's girlfriend, Fay?'

'Yah.'

Honestly. That girl is so thick-skinned. I didn't know what to do next. I could see the pirate ship with its big cross on the sails moored out in the bay. People go out there for a sort of big party – drink a lot of rum and do silly things. It would have been fun with Red.

I set off back to our rooms to get a towel and my script. I'd spend the afternoon learning it by the pool. And then it hit me like a sledgehammer. RED! Oh Red, what had I done? We only have two whole days left after today. Is he really angry? I couldn't even quite remember what we'd quarrelled over. Wasn't it all to do with him wanting me to forget about my parents for a while and concentrate on him? Well, I couldn't forget about them to order, could I? I mean, it's not every week you discover that your father has an appalling girlfriend and that your mother is going to have a baby, is it?

I let myself into our rooms and changed into my swimming gear. I didn't feel too great actually. Perhaps a quiet day away from everyone was what the doctor ordered. My brain was still a jumble of confused thoughts. Mum. Dad. Red. I felt alternately calm and then seething with anger. How could they? How could Red expect me to put them on one side? Why hadn't he passed on Oliver's message? How dare he think I'd make a fool of myself? I'd show him! I'd show them all!

I gathered up my script and towel and sunlotion and went down to the pool. I stretched out on a sunlounger under a beach umbrella and soon Maria's anguish blotted out my own. All the lines in the songs seemed so horribly relevant – I could *be* Maria. I could get under her skin all right. I under*stood* about love and families. Once he'd heard me, Oliver O'Neill wouldn't want anyone else.

By five o'clock I felt calm and focused. I went back to my room. I showered and changed into my surfie dress. It's flattering, but not over the top. I kept wondering if Red would phone, but he didn't. Perhaps Linden wasn't exaggerating – perhaps he *was* really upset with me. Well, I was pretty upset with him. Then again, perhaps he just wasn't back from the pirate ship.

By ten to six I kind of hoped Dad and Fay wouldn't come back before I went out. It would be far easier to leave them a note to explain. Fay would be bound to try and stop me. I spent five minutes working out what to put in the note and ended up writing: GONE OUT TO BAR, BACK BY NINE, LATEST. I even figured it might be good if someone started worrying if Oliver kept me out more than three hours.

I felt rather self-conscious waiting in Reception. Everyone else was passing through and I kept thinking Dad and Fay, or the Hayters, or even Red and Linden might walk in and wonder what I was doing. Well, I'd tell them, wouldn't I? I was pretty flattered that Oliver O'Neill thought I might have what it takes, wasn't I? I wasn't ashamed about talking to him about a part in his film, over a quiet drink.

At last, about half an hour late, I saw him approaching up the main drive. He looked dead cool in a pale linen suit and a dark casual shirt with trendy shades. And he was coming to take *me* out! I stood up so that he should see me. I could see him looking out for someone. I waved my script, but as I did that an ambulance came haring up the drive behind him. He jumped out of the way. The ambulance screeched to a halt and two ambulance men ran into reception. 'Room eleven!' they said. 'Bailey. Bianca Bailey.' They shot off in the direction of Bianca's rooms. What had happened? And then this tiny figure was brought down on a stretcher, an oxygen mask over her face.

'Bianca! What's happening?' I asked her mum, but

she was too distressed to listen to anyone other than Bianca and the ambulance men. I just had to stand back to let them through.

And then, from nowhere, Red appeared. 'Oh my God,' he said, watching what was going on. 'Is she all right?'

'I don't know, Red.'

And then Oliver came up to us both. He only addressed Red. 'I had myself a date with a hot little dancer called Dumont. Any idea which one she is?'

Red stood slightly in front of me. 'No, Dad,' he said, 'I haven't. I expect she thought better of it.' He looked back at me with a strange, cool expression, took his father's elbow and walked him towards the bar.

My legs felt weak. I crumpled onto one of the fancy sofas in the foyer. What had I done? What was Red thinking? And Bianca? What were they doing to her? Would they tell me? I couldn't bear it if she died. My headache was coming back. I felt claustrophobic – here, in the hotel!

I got to my feet and went out to the front of the hotel – I sat down on a wall in the shade of a sweetly smelling forangur tree. I tried to marshall my thoughts. Dad's girlfriend, Mum's baby – right now they were nothing to how I felt about Red and Bianca. I desperately wanted to talk to someone who would understand. Someone like Holly.

Without really thinking, I set off in the direction of the chalets Jonty had pointed out that first morning. Someone there would know where Holly was.

*

All I wanted was Holly. I forgot everything else. I walked on and on. After about ten minutes rainclouds gathered, and by the time I reached the place I was completely drenched. Like a mad old crone I went round the buildings peering in the windows. The boys slept four to a room, but all the rooms were empty. Finally I stood outside a room that was lit up against the wet evening. I pressed my face against the steamy window. They were in there, eating. All I had to do was get in.

I staggered round the outside of the building, looking for an entrance. I found one, went in and followed the sound of voices down a corridor until I came to their dining room. The door was open. I stood in the doorway, dripping. Suddenly the room went silent. 'Maddy!' Holly had seen me. 'Whatever's the matter?' She came over to where I was standing – and I knew no more.

When I came to, I was lying on her bed in the little room that she shared with Abby. Holly sat on Abby's bed. Someone had wrapped me in a blanket and made a sort of turban from a towel round my wet hair.

'Blimey, Maddy! You frightened the life out of me! You passed right out! What's going on? Mum's ringing your hotel, trying to get hold of your dad, but they can't find him.'

I sat up. I was warm and wet under the blanket. 'Could I borrow some dry clothes, Holly?' It was all I could think of. 'And I've got the curse – have you got any stuff?'

'Yes to both questions.' Holly was very practical. She found me a complete set of dry clothes – underwear, top, trousers, flip-flops, disappeared to the loo and came back telling me that I'd find everything I needed there. 'Sort yourself out and then come and talk to me. I'll get us a drink and something to eat.'

Food. When had I last eaten? Breakfast? Holly had made Marmite sandwiches. *Marmite sandwiches*! Bliss! And there was a weak orange squash! It was horrible and comforting and thirst-quenching all at the same time. One of the best meals of the whole holiday.

'Well, go on,' said Holly.

'I don't know where to begin,' I said.

'Anywhere,' said Holly. 'Work backwards.'

'I know that I really wanted to talk to you.'

'Why, especially?'

'Because Red gave me a look that shot icicles into my brain.'

'Why?'

'We had a row yesterday.'

'You and Red? I don't believe it!'

'He wanted me to be all cheerful and stop worrying about my parents.'

'What – your dad and Monstrous-Woman?'

'Them and – oh Holly, I've got so much to tell you!'

Holly's mum knocked on the door and came in. 'Hello, Madeleine.' She had a lovely soothing Scottish accent. 'I've left a message with the hotel for your father to ring us as soon as he gets in. But I'll be keeping you here until he comes in person to fetch you. I think you need a bit of looking after, dear.' She clucked sympathetically and backed out of the room.

'You were saying?' said Holly. 'Your dad and Monstrous-Woman—'

'Not just my dad. My mum as well. You see, *she* rang because she had some news for me, but we kept missing each other, and then I rang her and – and – her *news* was that she's pregnant again.'

'So irresponsible, these adults, aren't they?' said Holly, frowning but almost laughing. 'Is that such bad news? I thought you really adored your little sister? Babies are cute. I'd *love* to have a baby to play with!'

'I hadn't thought about the baby so much as its father. Roddy. He's a pain.'

'I thought he didn't live with you?'

'He doesn't. But I'm sure he will if there's a baby involved.'

'Face that one when you come to it. You've got a few months to blackmail everyone into making your room the perfect bedsit – you know, TV, kettle, futon, your own phone. Could be good.'

'Maybe. Holly, you're amazing. I *knew* you'd be able to help.'

'OK. So what else? As if that wasn't enough!'

'Well. I had the row with Red – yesterday, after we came off the submarine. Everyone was in a filthy mood. Then Linden cheesed me off by ringing up and saying that I'd really upset Red.'

'She's a liability, that girl.'

'Then, this morning I woke up with the curse and by the time I got up no one was around.'

'Our lot have been here all day, sorting ourselves out so that we can have a civilised last day tomorrow. I didn't even get to see Jonty. We're leaving early on Friday morning. Mum and Dad have said Charles and I can spend tomorrow evening with you and the Hayters, if we want, which is pretty cool of them. They know they'll get no peace if they don't let us!'

'Jonty and Dilly and the O'Neills all went on the pirate ship.'

'Lucky things! That's considered far too boozy for us "youngsters"!'

'*Anyway* . . .'

'You mean there's more?'

'Much more. I did this really stupid thing, you see. Linden's been winding me up about auditioning for Oliver O'Neill's *West Side Story*.'

'Wow! Do you think he'd give you a part?'

'That's the thing – no. Not really. But Linden's been saying things. Actually, Red said that his dad thought I might have "something" – after he'd seen the video of us dancing. But that was only because we'd had this misunderstanding when he saw me with the script. Oh, it's all so confusing, Holly. Red tells the truth, I know, but no one else does.'

'So what's the really stupid thing? I bet it wasn't that stupid!'

'I rang Oliver O'Neill on his mobile, told him I was a dancer, and arranged to meet him for a drink.'

'Ah. So it *was* that stupid.'

'In every possible way. But Holly – you know, I just wanted to do something for *me*. Everyone around me is so blooming selfish. I really believed he did want me to call him, though if I hadn't been so mixed up in the first place I'd never have done it. Anyway, needless to say, he thought I was some little bimbo groupie. He hadn't a clue who I was on the phone. Do you know what he said to Red? He said – "I had myself a date with a hot little dancer called Dumont"!'

'It was a close thing then.'

'Yup.'

'So do I gather Red was none too pleased at you arranging a cosy little rendezvous with his father?'

'He just looked daggers at me. But do you know what actually got in the way of me meeting up with Oliver O'Neill? I mean, thank goodness it did – I was way out of my depth – but it was awful – an ambulance coming for Bianca. They brought her down all wired up, and I don't know if I can see her at the hospital, or what.'

'Tell you what,' said Holly. 'Let's get my mum. You know she's a nurse – she might know the score on Bianca. In fact, let's get phoning. I'm going to phone Red.'

'You what?'

'I'm going to tell him you're here and you're in a state and you're not coming back till tomorrow and that you're upset and that there have been all sorts of misunderstandings but that you're still completely potty about him. How's that?'

'Potty?'

'Uhuh.'

'Oh. OK. Thank you Holly.'

'Good. That's that settled then. Here, write down his mobile number for me. I'm sure you know it off by heart. Mu-um?'

Holly's Mum bustled in. 'What is it, dear?'

'Tell Mum about Bianca, Mads.'

'Is this the little leukaemia girl?'

Holly went off to phone Red, and her Mum told me all about leukaemia patients and how they sometimes got infections, and that it sounded as if that had happened to Bianca, but that it didn't necessarily mean she was about to die. She was so kind – I couldn't imagine her moaning about all the rich people or suggesting that Jonty wasn't right for Holly. But that's other people's mothers for you, isn't it? With people like Holly and her mum around, the world isn't such a bad place. I realised how at home I felt – it was quite a relief to be with *normal* people for a change! What's more, the rain had stopped raining and the evening sky was clear and full of stars.

I heard the phone ringing and Holly answering. She passed the call on to her mum and came back in. 'Right. Well, that was your dad. You'd left them a note apparently, saying you'd be back by nine. He'd just started to worry when he picked up the message at reception. I've put him on to Mum. She's determined that you're going to stay here tonight.'

'What about Abby?'

'Oh, Mum's already moved her in with the other little girl.'

'So I just stay here?'

'That's right. Shame we couldn't do it for longer!'

'Holly, we really will meet up at home won't we?'

'I hope so. By the way, do you know someone called Hannah Gross?' Holly asked.

How funny. A picture of Hannah and her anxious face floated into my mind. She and Sophie and Charlotte seemed to belong in another life. 'Hannah Gross! Of course I do, she's one of my best friends. Why?'

'Oh, some of my friends go to her school and they're all going on a music course together. I thought she lived over your way.'

'Wow, what a coincidence!'

'That's London schools for you. Someone always knows someone. Anyway, Maddy – we're forgetting the *important* phone conversation.'

I knew I was putting it off. 'OK. What did he say?'

Holly held the thumb and little finger of her right hand to her ear. ' *"Red? Hi, It's Holly."*

"Holly. Hi! What's up? Is Maddy with you" (See – he cares!)

"She's staying over, Red, with us. She's OK now, but she passed out earlier."

"She WHAT? Is she OK? I mean, can I come over and see her?"

'I thought I'd lay it on a bit. *"Well, I don't think she ought to see anyone just now Red. She's been through emotional hell."* '

'You said *that*, Holly?'

'Yup. Well, you have been through emotional hell. I know you have. Anyway, it had the desired effect.'

She held the imaginary phone to her ear again. 'This is Red. *"I know she's pretty upset about her parents. But hey, we've all been through it—"*

"Maybe, Red, but she's upset about you, too, and all this business with your dad. She'd no idea Linden had set her up. She feels terrible."

"I feel awful bad about that. I should have told her straight out – Dad only deals with agents. I guess it's a world I understand, but how could she? Holly, are you sure I can't come over?"

"No Red. Certainly not now my mum's on the case."

"Which reminds me. Bianca. I suppose Maddy's scared about her, too?"

"As if she wasn't feeling bad enough already." I wasn't going to let him off, Maddy.'

I was beginning to feel sorry for Red at Holly's hands. 'Couldn't he come over, Holly?'

'Absolutely not. I'm not joking, Maddy. You've been through enough today. Let him sweat a bit. Anyway, my mum couldn't possibly say No to your dad but Yes to Red, now could she?'

'So what did he say then?'

'He said, *"Tell her I'm real sorry, Holly. Tell her I can't wait to see her. Tell her – no don't, I'll tell her that myself when I see her. She will be back in the morning won't she?"*

"She will, Red."

"Tell her to call me if she feels up to it. I so want to talk to her."

"OK, Red, I'll tell her. Bye!" ' And she put her imaginary phone down. 'So, I'd say you have nothing to worry about. And don't you *dare* call him. You want

the upper hand, remember?' She stood up and read-
justed the hairband round her ponytail. 'The boys
have a snack before bedtime – d'you want to come
and join us?'

I could get used to this well organised institutional
life. How am I ever going to get used to slumming it
with Mum – *pregnant* Mum – again?

Fourteen

In the morning Holly's mum woke us with a cup of tea.
It was wonderful. She sat on Holly's bed while we
drank it. 'Right, girls,' she said, 'I've been on the phone
to Maddy's father and he'll be over in about an hour –
so you can have breakfast with us, Maddy. And I've
also rung the hospital to see if there's any news on wee
Bianca. I had a word with her mother, and she says the
child's stable for the present. You can visit this afternoon if you want, but sadly she'll have to stay put until
she's strong enough to fly home to a hospital in
England. Poor wee mite.'

My clothes had dried in the early morning sun.
They were lovely and warm and slightly crisp when I
put them on. I even enjoyed having cereals for
breakfast. I was dying to phone Red, but since there
was only one payphone in the place I didn't get the
chance. Before I knew it, Dad had come for me in a

taxi. On his own. Holly's mum brought him to our room. She'd obviously had a word or two with him (it's clear she thinks he's hopelessly irresponsible) – his expression was one of concern. I was so pleased to see him. 'Daddy!' I gave him a huge hug. He clung on to me.

'Sweetheart,' he said in the taxi, 'Whatever's been going on? You must tell me!'

So I decided to tell it how it was. I told him all about being upset by him and Fay, by Mum being pregnant, my row with Red and the decision to call Oliver O'Neill, and being saved, as it were, by the ambulance coming for Bianca.

'And I just wasn't there for you, was I? I do sometimes think I wasn't cut out for fatherhood. Has it all gone *horribly* wrong?'

'I think Red understands now. Holly told him everything.'

'I'm pretty disgusted by Oliver's behaviour.'

'Always someone worse than yourself, eh, Dad?'

'Well, he told me himself that he was impressed by your dancing.'

'Which of course is quite a different thing from working with professional casting agents. I should have known myself, Dad – even at my Saturday morning place we're dead professional when it comes to auditions and casting. I don't know what came over me.'

'Well don't punish yourself too hard. I'd say it was an understandable mistake. I blame him. Hot little date, eh? I'd like to give him a piece of mind.'

'Well don't, Dad. That will only make matters a million times worse, and he *is* Red's father.'

'So how are the young lovers? I'd say you were faring marginally better than the old ones on current showing.'

We were pulling up outside the hotel. I saw it with fresh eyes – like a palace for the incredibly privileged. Dad *had* brought me here as his little princess. He hadn't wanted to spoil that first week by talking about Fay. Maybe he'd known in his heart of hearts it wouldn't work out with her. I gave him a quick kiss before we got out. 'Love you, Dad. I'm fine now. It's all been brilliant, really.'

'Go and sort it out with Romeo. Look, he's over there, waiting for you.' Do you know, I hadn't noticed Red standing outside the entrance? And when I looked at him, before he saw me, he seemed smaller somehow, diminished.

'Maddy!' He rushed over and caught me up in his arms. I recoiled slightly. He stood back. 'Maddy – we are OK aren't we?'

'Sure,' I said lightly. I *wasn't* a hundred per cent sure, though. 'Red, let me just go up to my room, have a shower and stuff. I'm feeling kind of icky.'

He looked wary. 'OK. Sure,' he said, nodding. 'See you down by the pool?'

'Somewhere cool and shady.'

'I'll find a spot by the fountains.'

'Give me an hour.'

I had to get my head straight. It wasn't so simple to

forget that I *had* been angry with Red. But then, he'd only been wanting us to enjoy our time together, hadn't he? Bit like Dad, really, not wanting to mention Fay. Both of them just wanting to live for the present.

If Red wasn't to blame, why did I suddenly not feel so enthusiastic about being with him? My hormones might have had something to do with it. But it wasn't just that . . . Of course! That was it! We'd had our first row! We'd become human and the magic had worn off a little. Red has an ego and pride, weaknesses, confusions. I hadn't noticed them before. Our romance so far had just been a series of sunsets and kissing. A real holiday romance – the genuine article. But was that *all* it had been?

I put a sarong over my bikini and sat at the dressing table to dry my hair. I'd been totally *in love* with Red, blindly in love. And now that bubble had burst and I wasn't sure whether I *loved* him or not. There is a distinction, isn't there?

I packed my beach bag. There was a small paper bag at the bottom. It was the ring I'd bought Red in the market – I'd never had the chance to give it to him! Maybe I never would. I was completely, utterly confused. I set off for the fountains.

Red had bagged us a couple of sunbeds. He looked as hunky as ever in his swimming shorts – I wasn't going to have to *pretend* to find him attractive! Though I did notice, as I hadn't before, that his blond eyebrows nearly met in the middle and that his hands were smaller and neater than I remembered.

He had a cold drink all lined up for me, too – still thoughtful. 'They've got it all mapped out for us – can you believe it?'

'Who? What?'

'The Hayters. For Dilly's and Jonty's last day with Charles and Holly. Afternoon out on a boat – you know, the sort you can swim from, and dinner this evening – at that place where the turtles come up the beach. Steel band. The Hayters want to pay for you and me too. And Linden.'

'Where is Linden?'

'Keeping her distance from me I expect.'

'Why?'

'*Why*?'

'Should I know?'

'Maddy – she only did her best to upset us both – all that about messages from my dad. She played one game too many and I told her just to keep out of my way for a while!' Was Red putting too much of the blame on Linden? I didn't know. All I knew was that I couldn't take anything at face value any more.

'Won't that be a bit awkward this evening then?'

'We'll make sure it's not!' Red put his arm round me and tried to kiss me, but somehow we couldn't get comfortable.

'I can't go on a boat this afternoon, Red. I want to visit Bianca.'

'So would I, if I'd known it was on the cards,' he said. He sat up. 'Maddy. I want you to look me in the eye.' I tried. It wasn't easy. Red's face was troubled. 'Something's changed, hasn't it, Maddy? I recognise the signs. I'm not stupid, you know.'

Tears came into my eyes. 'Red, I'm sorry. Believe me – I don't know what's changed. I only know it has. We were on such a high. Now – just knowing it's got to end . . .'

Red looked away. I knew I had hurt him by not responding like I used to. 'I thought . . . that maybe . . . somehow . . .' he trailed off. I had to hug him, make things better between us. 'Don't do that unless you mean it,' he said, trying to shake me off.

'Red?' It was my turn. 'Now I want you to look me in the eye.' He tried, but he blinked a lot. 'Listen. Perhaps it's better this way. We were going to be separated in a couple of days, whatever happened. Can we just spend the rest of our time together kind of – starting again? As if we'd been parted and then met up again as holiday romance couples do? Only for them, seeing each other in some dreary old town in the rain, it's almost always a disappointment. For us, it's just that we know we're both human, warts and all – and we can be just a bit more realistic? Please Red?'

He wasn't' going to make this easy. 'But Maddy – I'm still crazy about you. Nothing's changed for me. Nothing apart from your feelings.'

'Red – I know you don't think all this stuff about my parents is important—'

'I do now – honestly. I feel real bad about how I trivialised it. I just felt *we* were so much more important, and our time together was so short—' I caught his eye, and before I knew it, we were kissing, desperately, and both our faces were wet with tears. Good job the fountains were so close by. 'OK,' he said after a while. 'Let's start again. Maybe I like this idea.'

'I'm more confused than ever now, but maybe I do too. Let's see Bianca, go to dinner with the Hayters, have a fabulous day tomorrow and—' I looked at him. I liked his funny eyebrows. I liked his sensitive hands. 'I think I'm crazy about you all over again.' We kind of stopped talking for a while after that.

Bianca lay in a large cot in a bright ward where the walls were covered in children's paintings. A breeze blew the muslin curtains at the window and nurses and children clattered about, almost drowning out the large TV that blared away in the corner. Bianca was asleep, breathing lightly. Her parents looked exhausted.

'I'm afraid you won't be able to see her tomorrow,' said her mother. 'They've got to do a biopsy under anaesthetic, so you'll have to say your goodbyes today.'

What a shock. I had no idea how I was going to get through the next few minutes. I sat down by the oversized cot. One side had been let down. 'Bianca, sweetheart?' I whispered, stroking her hair. She shifted and half opened her eyes.

'Maddthy!' she slurred. 'Have you come to read to me?'

'Yes, angel,' I lied. And then, so it wasn't a lie – 'I've come to tell you the story of Bianca and the Banana Boat.'

'Goodth,' she said, closing her eyes again and smiling. 'I like that one.'

Fighting against the sadness that was choking me, I began. 'Once upon a time there was a beautiful little girl called Bianca who loved bananas.' (Was that the best I could do?) 'She ate bananas for breakfast, bananas for lunch and bananas for tea. That was because she loved everything to be bright yellow like the sun. Bright yellow made her feel happy. But best of all, she liked to cool down by going out on the Banana Boat. Out there in the sun and the wind she felt free as a bird, racing, flying through the rainbow spray . . .' And then I found myself softly singing, 'Hold my hand, I'll take you there . . .' instead of finishing the story. Bianca's hand lay limply in mine. She was asleep again, her little face delicate and peaceful. I couldn't have gone on anyway – I was crying too hard and my voice just wouldn't come out. I released my hand, kissed my fingertips and planted them on her forehead. 'Bye Bianca,' I said, and rushed out of the ward before she woke up and saw my tears.

Red came out a few minutes later and joined me on the bench in the hospital corridor. We held each other and cried and cried and cried.

'Let's go outside,' Red managed to say. 'We're upsetting people.'

The hospital was in town, but it had a small garden where we could sit together in the shade. There was nothing much we could say. The cruelty of knowing that we would never see that smashing little girl again, ever, was more than either of us could bear.

But there did come a time, after an hour or so, when we both felt all cried out. Red looked at his watch. 'We've got a couple of hours until this dinner. What's the best thing for us to do?'

'I keep telling myself that she's still alive. It's not fair on her for us to behave as if she's just died, is it?'

Red looked at me, as if to say, but that's how it is.

'I have to believe that maybe I'll be able to write to her or talk on the phone or something once she comes back to England.'

Red carried on looking at me. We both knew that Bianca had very little time to live. And then I had a thought. 'Red – let's go back to our rooms. I'm going to do just that – write to Bianca. I want to. I'll tell her all about what we're going to do tonight and about what we're going to wear and everything – just as if she was Lo-lo. That's what she'd want to know. And I'll tell her about the new baby and how Dad and Fay probably won't stay together. And I'll tell her about Holly and Jonty—'

Red pulled my head onto his chest. 'Do it,' he said, and then, quietly into my hair, he whispered, 'I love you, Maddy.'

We walked to the cab rank. 'Will you write me letters like that? E-mails?'

'You won't be as far away as she is,' I said.

Dinner was a laugh. Looking back I wouldn't have thought it possible to go from one such extreme to another, but, thank goodness, it was. I was living for the present. Sometimes you have to. How else do people cope with grief lurking around the corner? I was with Red all the way for simply enjoying the time we had together, though our relationship had definitely entered a different and deeper phase. But dealing with saying goodbye to Bianca had somehow prepared me for saying goodbye to Red. Holly, Jonty, Dilly and Charles all knew they would be able to see each other again, though there was plenty of kissing and crying at the end.

Red and I spent Friday on the beach. Linden hung around with Dilly and Jonty and didn't bother us. It was as if we were survivors and she knew she couldn't touch us. We bumped into Red's father in the bar before dinner. I was terrified he'd make the connection, but Red reassured me that 'his son's girlfriend Maddy' and a 'hot little dancer called Dumont' wouldn't come under the same category in his father's highly compartmentalised brain. 'Do you two want to have a drink with me?'

'Come on Mads,' said Red. 'Take your mind off things.' So we had a very civilised drink with Oliver O'Neill, and he asked all sorts of fatherly questions about school and home and my family. He even looked at the two of us and said – 'And how are you two lovebirds going to cope when cruel fate tears you apart?'

'Dad!' said Red, embarrassed.

'No, I mean it,' said Oliver. 'I'm not scared to mention it. It's obvious that you two are crazy about each other. I was wondering if we should invite the young lady over the US of A some time?'

Red was still embarrassed. 'We'll just have to see, won't we, dad.'

'Well, you're such great kids. I'd hate to see either of you pining away. I'm just saying it could be arranged. Don't be afraid to ask, son.'

'OK Dad. Thanks.'

'Thanks Mr O'Neill,' I said.

'Call me Oliver, please.'

Red and I sat out in our favourite place under the stars. Dad said I had to be in by eleven because of our early start and in a funny sort of way I was glad to know the limits on our time. 'I wonder where Bianca is now,' I said.

Red knows my lines better than I do. 'About half way there, I should say. And where are we?'

'I've done so much thinking, Red. I'm getting quite philosophical in my old age. Bianca's parents will have to think of her whole life as a sort of bright capsule of time. And that's how I think of this holiday with you. For a while nothing touched us, did it? And then my stupid parents got in the way. But then, when Bianca did too, she kind of made it richer, more intense. I can't quite describe what I mean.'

'You're doing good,' said Red. 'Go on.'

'Well, our time together is like this bright little light. It won't go away. I can't even think of saying goodbye to you, but I know that little light will always be there, bobbing along with Bianca's. And we'll write. And then one day we'll see each other again, and – and—'

'I don't want to talk any more, Maddy. I can't hold

you in a letter. We've got just half an hour to make more memories.'

Red and I said goodbye that night. It was a bit like with Bianca. It was good to know that we were still in the same building for a while longer. In the morning Dad and Fay and I went to the airport together, though Fay was on a different flight from us, thank goodness. They said all the right things to each other when they parted, but it seemed pretty unemotional to me. All these goodbyes – I hadn't forgotten that soon *I'd* be saying goodbye to Dad again too. I remembered how upset I'd been when he said Red was just a holiday romance, but he was my father. Dad goes away, but he always comes back, some time.

I thought about my 'holiday romance' and how I'd process it for the others when we got together at the end of the holidays. The romance with Red had been so perfect, but it had been balanced in a subtle and complex way between a 'romance' with Dad, and another with Bianca. And I was forgetting. There was someone else. More constant than all the others. Holly. I'd made a terrific new girl friend, who would still be around when I got home. Because, when it comes down to it, aren't your female friends more important than anyone?

That's a difficult one. Because with Red I touched on *love* in a way that I never have before. Already I reach out and find that he is missing. Nothing's quite as bright as it was when he was around. And however much I hold onto that little bubble of light, right now it's not enough. I twist a funny little necklace round my finger. It is a present from Red – three beads on a thread: a gold one for me, a red one for him – and a white one for Bianca. He bought it for me outside the hospital that afternoon. And of course I gave him the ring. At first I worried that I'd bought it on that awful day of the submarine, but then I thought it was good, because it was a reminder of the time we discovered we were human after all.

Epilogue

The sleepover was at Hannah's house. First I had to read to Lo-lo and play Barbados with her Barbies. I talked to her a lot about a little girl called Bianca. Bianca died two weeks ago after making it home. Her parents wrote to me. I keep their letter with some photos of her and the video that Red sent. The video is completely brilliant, especially the underwater stuff! Red is a genius as well as everything else. I miss him like anything, but somehow he's already part of the past. Then I made Mum a cup of tea and left her sitting in front of the TV. Roddy hasn't moved in yet, and his technical support job means that he often works in the evenings, all of which is fine by me. I'm working subtly on the bedsit scheme. Mum is really pleased about the baby and Lo-lo seems quite intrigued by the whole thing. I have this sentimental desire for it to be called Bianca if it's a girl.

I finally got my make-up on and loaded on the Hugo Boss. My tan seems to be fading fast. I've already made contact with Hannah and Charlotte, though I haven't said much about Barbados, I was too gutted about Bianca. Sophie's the one I'm most interested in, anyway.

'Maddeeeee!' There was a squeal as I crossed the road

and Sophie was on the other side, waving frantically. I threw my arms around her.

We quickly compared forearms. 'Your tan is fresher, that's not fair!' I said.

'But yours is pretty incredible, Maddy,' said Sophie. 'So go on, then! Spill the beans!'

'Well, Hannah met a guy called Jonny, I think, and Charlotte hasn't said much – not that I think there'll be much to say!'

'No, idiot! You! What happened to you? Was he gorgeous?'

'What makes you think I met anyone?'

'Stop teasing! You always meet someone. You only have to go on the bus to meet someone!'

'Yes, he was gorgeous. So what about yours?'

'Well, he was gorgeous too, but – it was complicated.'

'So was mine. Though really it was everything else that was complicated. And something really really sad happened too.'

'Oh Maddy!'

We'd reached Hannah's mansion (it is, compared to our place). 'Yeah, well. I haven't got over it yet. But I'll tell you more some other time, on your own, OK?'

'OK.' We rang on the doorbell and waited for Hannah to come and let us in. 'I'm dying to know what happened to the others. I bet it was more than you give them credit for, especially Hannah with her Jonny. She's a sneaky one!'

'Well, I'm going to quiz Charlotte about that Josh. It seems he might be coming to London next term.'

'So what about your gorgeous guy in Barbados?'

'He lives in America, doesn't he? And he's the one that taught me to live for the present – because, well, you never know what's going to happen to people do you?'

Also in the *GIRLS LIKE YOU QUARTET*:

Four girls, four lives, one summer.

It was Maddy's idea that all four of them should have holiday romances and report back at the end of the summer.

These are their stories . . .

Sophie

Blonde, drop-dead beautiful Sophie is used to getting her own way, and not worrying about the broken hearts she leaves behind. She's determined that a family camping holiday in France is not going to cramp her style. What's more she knows exactly who she wants . . . but does he feel the same way about her?

Hannah

Hannah is the clever one, and hard to please – but she's really shy too. She doesn't fancy her chances on a summer music course – so she decides that the boys are just not worth bothering about . . . not any of them . . . or are they?

Charlotte

Shy, dreamy Charlotte has been going to the Lake District every year for as long as she can remember and she's loved Josh from afar for as long. But this year she's going without her older sister. It might be the chance she's been waiting for. What if Josh notices her – just because she's four years younger than him – it doesn't mean all her dreams won't come true – does it?